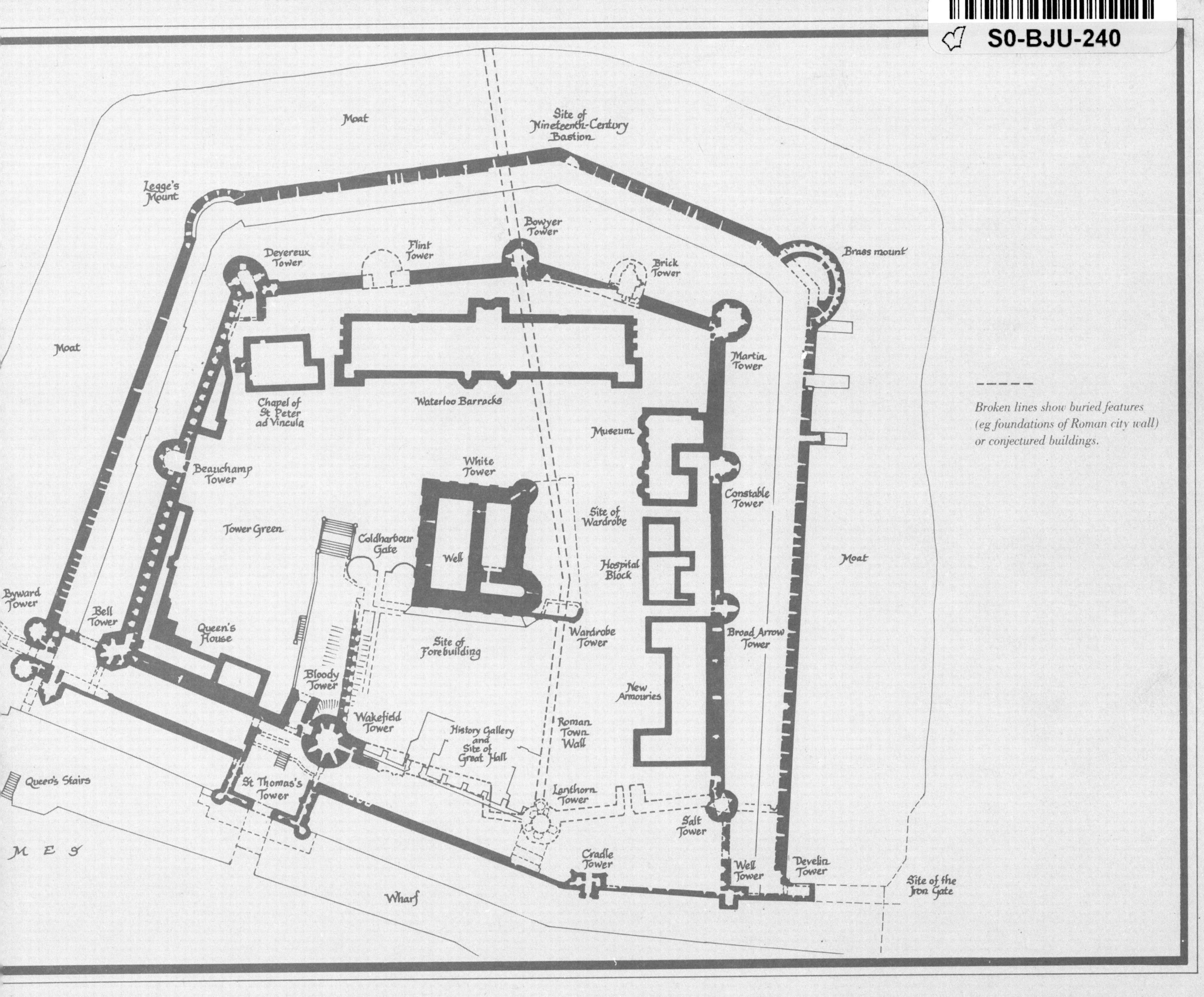
Moat
Site of Nineteenth-Century Bastion
Legge's Mount
Bowyer Tower
Flint Tower
Devereux Tower
Brick Tower
Brass mount
Moat
Martin Tower
Chapel of St Peter ad Vincula
Waterloo Barracks
Broken lines show buried features (eg foundations of Roman city wall) or conjectured buildings.
Museum
White Tower
Beauchamp Tower
Constable Tower
Site of Wardrobe
Tower Green
Coldharbour Gate
Well
Hospital Block
Moat
Byward Tower
Bell Tower
Queen's House
Wardrobe Tower
Broad Arrow Tower
Site of Forebuilding
Bloody Tower
New Armouries
Wakefield Tower
History Gallery and Site of Great Hall
Roman Town Wall
Queen's Stairs
St Thomas's Tower
Lanthorn Tower
Salt Tower
M E S
Cradle Tower
Well Tower
Develin Tower
Site of the Iron Gate
Wharf

THE TOWER OF LONDON

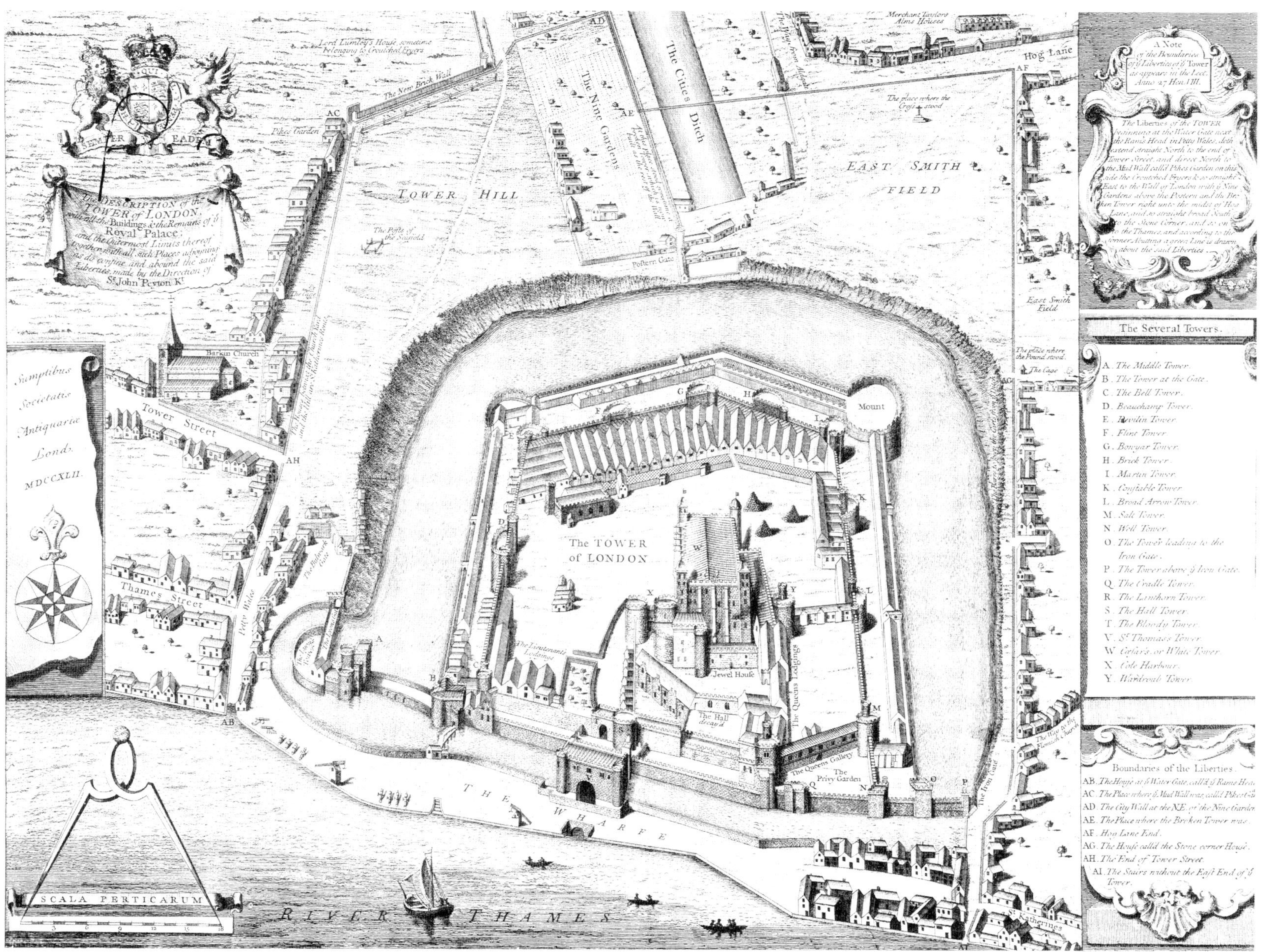

The invaluable 1597 plan by Haiward and Gascoyne, the first authentic picture of the Tower. See page 34.

THE TOWER OF LONDON

AN ILLUSTRATED HISTORY

RUSSELL CHAMBERLIN

With photographs by
SIMON MCBRIDE

First published in Great Britain in 1989 by
Webb & Bower (Publishers) Limited,
5 Cathedral Close, Exeter, Devon EX1 1EZ,
in association with Michael Joseph Limited,
27 Wright's Lane, London W8 5TZ

Penguin Books Ltd, Registered Offices: Harmondsworth, Middlesex, England
Viking Penguin Inc, 40 West 23rd Street, New York, New York 10010, USA
Penguin Books Australia Ltd, Ringwood, Victoria, Australia
Penguin Books Canada Ltd, 2801 John Street, Markham, Ontario, Canada L3R 1D4
Penguin Books (NZ) Ltd, 182–190 Wairau Road, Auckland 10, New Zealand

Designed by Ron Pickless
Plans drawn by Malcolm Couch
Production by Nick Facer/Rob Kendrew

Black and white picture research by Anne-Marie Ehrlich

British Library Cataloguing in Publication Data

Chamberlin, Russell.
The Tower of London: an illustrated
history.
1. London. Tower Hamlet, (London Borough).
Castles: Tower of London, history.
942.1'5

ISBN 0–86350–189–3

Typeset in Great Britain by J&L Composition Ltd, Filey, North Yorkshire

Colour reproduction by Peninsular Repro Service Ltd, Exeter, Devon

Printed and bound in Great Britain by Purnell Book Production Limited, Paulton, Bristol

Contents

PROLOGUE
THE FORT BY THE RIVER

10.45 of a soft, cloudy, summer, Sunday morning. Already there is a handful of tourists gathering around the entrance although the public is not admitted until 2pm. The gates of the Middle Tower are open, but two scarlet-clad Guardsmen courteously but firmly direct the curious away. They inspect me closely as I approach – 'I want to go to the service in St Peter's', nod politely and step to one side, and I enter the Tower of London.

Inside, there is a cool stillness, the towering grey walls trapping the silence, cutting off the roar of London. The towers drift past, each with its piece of history, mostly tragic: the Byward Tower, the Bell Tower, St Thomas's Tower, the Bloody Tower. But it's not all history. Moving as softly as a cat in his high, lace-up boots, clad in combat fatigue, a young soldier appears round the corner of the Bloody Tower. Slung over his shoulder is no halberd or crossbow but an efficient, rather sinister-looking, automatic rifle. I pass two more such soldiers. They are not standing stiffly at attention like so many mechanized dolls but are prowling silently, purposefully. One is reminded again, as one will be reminded again and yet again, that this is still Her Majesty's Tower of London, royal palace, garrison and, if need be, prison.

Up the steps: past the site of the scaffold and so on into the church of St Peter Ad Vincula, the Tower's own parish church. Macaulay called this the saddest place in the world and he did not exaggerate, but on this summer's morning, with the diffused sunlight streaming through the windows on to the gleaming brass and massed flowers, it is at once elegant and gay, Tudor architecture at its very best. The floor of ancient flagstones is highly polished: inescapably one's attention is drawn towards them, wondering exactly what lies beneath.

A Yeoman Warder conducts visitors to seats and by about 11 o'clock there are about a dozen of us, most quite obviously residents of the great castle but one or two, like myself, strayed in from the outside world. At 11am a bell booms: again, imagination takes over, wondering how often its predecessor must have boomed, carrying a more sinister message. As the strokes cease, the Chaplain sweeps in, resplendent in the scarlet robes of a Chapel Royal. The organist follows, equally splendid in the gown and furred hood of his academic order. There then comes a flood of white and scarlet, the choir, including four women wearing rather fetching seventeenth-century bonnets.

Matins begins and proceeds on its time-honoured way with the sunlight speckling the floor, the choir incredibly powerful and stirring, the great organ filling the silences in between. The Yeoman Warder reads the First Lesson. It's from Jeremiah and he presents it like an NCO making a report, clear, crisp, factual. The Psalms follow, incantations of an Oriental tribe transformed into Jacobean English, intoned in the twentieth century as though new minted. The Yeoman Warder suddenly appears with a great silver mace of a startlingly modern design and stops by one of the pews where a middle-aged, authoritative-looking man has sat unobtrusively throughout. The Governor of the Tower of London arises, advances to the lectern behind the mace, reads the Second Lesson, returns to his seat. The service continues: more psalms, hymn and sermon with a raven outside seeming to make ironic comment, its harsh croak at times almost drowning the Chaplain's gentle voice. Announcements as in any other parish church. Next week there will be Communion in William the Conqueror's massive chapel in the White Tower itself; tickets are available for a celebration; the collection.

We file out. The Governor enters into an altercation with a

Yeomen Warders in full ceremonial dress attend a church parade

raven, probably the one that has been commenting on the sermon. It has apparently strayed off its patch and he tries, without much success, to shoo it away. A lady member of the congregation lends her umbrella which he opens and then he advances rather warily on the great bird. Sullenly, it hops away and one suddenly appreciates those notices warning visitors that these intelligent creatures with their massive beaks can be dangerous.

So, to retrace one's steps: past that simple cobbled square where two queens lost their heads: past the immense White Tower: under the arch of the Bloody Tower where Walter Raleigh ate out his heart for thirteen years, so back to the outside world as the clock strikes noon.

2pm and the queue for the ticket office stretches far back along the moat. There must be at least a thousand people in it, the first comers of the six thousand or so who will pass through the Middle

The main entrance: the Middle Tower seen from within the arch of the Byward Tower

Opposite Moat, bridge and exterior of the Byward Tower. The moat was drained in the early nineteenth century.

Tower by the end of that Sunday, a moiety of the 2.3 million who will enter the Tower of London over the next twelve months. There is a remarkable ethnic mix. Asiatics are the most obvious, Japanese for the most part, quiet, neat, festooned with gleaming electronic equipment. Boisterous young Germans, casually dressed, very clean, many laden with the rucksacks out of which they seem to live. French, Italians, many Americans, curiously few Africans or Arabs. Immediately ahead of me is a family from one of the northern counties. He is startled and a bit put out by the price of admission: '£4 each for us; £2 for the kids. Twelve quid altogether.' She comforts him by pointing out that they can spend the rest of the day in the Tower without paying for anything else. Both discuss, disapprovingly, the squalid appearance of the public square in front of the great monument. 'You'd think somebody would sweep up once in a while. And there's nowhere to eat except for that little stall.' Their son, about ten years old, is agog for the sights that await them. 'Shall we see where they cut people's heads off?' The queen's crown comes under discussion. 'Is it the real one?' The consensus is that it must be.

The queue shuffles on. At the Middle Tower there is a thorough examination of baggage. Nothing perfunctory about this for the Tower is a prime terrorist target: in 1974 an IRA bomb exploded in the basement of the White Tower, killing one unfortunate woman, wounding several people. Within the precincts the queue disintegrates, its members going individual ways, flooding into every area that is open to the public. Many coalesce around one or the other of the Yeomen Warders who conduct informal mini-tours. One is aware of being constantly under surveillance for the Warders are everywhere: invariably courteous, seemingly infinitely patient but with a kind of jovial toughness underneath. For all their comic-opera uniform these are veteran soldiers and look it.

By 4pm it is impossible to move against the tide through any of the public rooms, and the open spaces are as crowded as the beach of a seaside resort. The queue outside the Jewel House waiting to see the regalia curves back and forward on itself like a great serpent: almost every step of the stairs leading to the upper storey of the Bloody Tower has someone on it: people are standing virtually shoulder to shoulder along the dozen or so yards of Raleigh's Walk. In the Armoury a woman tries to move against the crowd with a child in a pushchair, is mutinous when politely but firmly directed to go the right way round, eventually obeys with a bad grace. She is a rarity, for the crowd, consisting very largely of family groups, is singularly well behaved: no yobs, of course, for they would be very rapidly dealt with: but no consumers of fast food whose activities usually mark every public open-air place: no bizarre costumes.

At 5.30 a burst of music over the loudspeakers heralds the warning that the Tower will close in fifteen minutes' time. The Warders begin the long process of shepherding people towards the main gate. A woman comes out of one of the lodgings in the Casemates with two large dogs, setting them free in the moat to race and burn up energy. From another lodging a man emerges with pipe and shirt-sleeved comfort. There is a general air of unbuttoning, relaxing, as the last of the thousands pass through the Middle Tower and the great, black, wooden gates quietly swing to.

9.30 of a black January night. Our little group outside the iron gates is islanded in a pool of light: beyond is darkness and silence, the City of London settling into sleep. At 9.45 a figure emerges from the darkness of the Middle Tower, approaches us and gives a few crisp instructions. One of the group, an American, has a large camera. The Warder turns sharply upon him and brusquely, almost rudely, says 'The Ceremony of the Keys is not an entertainment. No camera. No tape recordings. Understand?' Chastened, the American puts his camera away and we follow obediently through the Middle Tower where we are handed over to a scarlet-clad figure: the Watchman in a great coat that descends to his ankles. He backs us up behind a line in front of the Traitors' Gate and explains the complex series of movements that will take place over the next quarter of an hour. 'The Chief Warder will meet the Escort under the Bloody Tower arch there, while I go back to the Byward Tower. The Chief Warder, with the Keys, will come to meet me, locking up the gates there. He'll then return to this spot where he'll be challenged. Don't you move from here till I tell you.'

We stand dutifully as the ballet begins, going through an archaic sequence supposedly unbroken over the centuries. They say that in the Second World War the blast of a bomb swept the entire party off its feet until the Chief Warder, an elderly man, rose and said tetchily, 'Come on, we've got to finish the job'. Nothing happens tonight and the Ceremony proceeds smoothly, archaic with its lantern and fancy-dress costume: ridiculous in that the Gates will have to be opened to let us out – but deeply moving. The Chief Warder is challenged by the young sentry at the Bloody Tower: 'Halt. Who comes there?' 'The Keys.' 'Whose Keys?' 'Queen Elizabeth's Keys.' 'Advance, Queen Elizabeth's Keys. All's well.' Escort and Keys pass through the arch of the Bloody Tower, the Watchman beckons us forward then halts us at the foot of the flight of steps. Half-way up the steps a detachment of Guards present Arms. The Chief Warder takes two precise paces forward, raises his bonnet, proclaims 'God preserve Queen Elizabeth'. Guard and Escort answer 'Amen', a clock begins to strike the hour and, exactly on the first note, a bugle rises up in the haunting melody of the Last Post. One more day in the vast tally of the Tower's days is at an end.

The Tower of London faithfully reflects the history of a great nation over a period of nearly a thousand years. In 1244, a captive Welsh prince fell to his death while trying to escape from the White Tower: in 1941, a leading Nazi joined the hundreds who had heard the clang and clash of a door closing and a lock turning, separating him from the living, outside world.

The last execution in the Tower took place not in the sixteenth century, but at 7.15am on 15 August 1941 when a spy was shot in the moat. Until this century, the Tower was the depository for most public records, guarding what was, in effect, the memory of the nation preserved in parchment and paper. It is still the repository for the regalia in which is vested the mystique of sovereignty of one of the world's oldest monarchies.

It has been a 'tourist attraction' since at least the sixteenth century: in 1599 the German, Thomas Platter, bitterly complained about being mulcted no less than eight times for tips. It is also a living community with the longest, recorded continuity of occupation in Europe and, perhaps, the world. Long before the palace of the Popes began to rise on the Vatican Hill: long before the Louvre was commenced, or Schönbrunn, people were attempting to make themselves comfortable in the stone monster just as, today, their successors attempt to lead a normal life between the flood-tides of tourists.

Bishop Abel whiled away an hour or so carving this rebus of his name

Above The queue for the Jewel House

Left Hoisting the flag at sunrise

Top Last post *Opposite* Sunset

Those who have passed through the Tower, whether as master or as victim or simply as worker, are innumerable. Some idea of the number and variety of prisoners alone can be gained from the dozens of bored, resigned, or agonized inscriptions gouged in the walls of the Beauchamp Tower – some whose names resound in history, others known to no one but their immediate contemporaries. Within the scope of the present book, any attempt to identify the myriads even by name and occupation, to provide even an outline of all the dramas and tragedies that have been played out behind those looming walls would result in little more than a catalogue. The figures and events chosen here are those which not only have an intrinsic interest, but which throw light upon their own times as exemplars. Certain 'set pieces', certain tragic figures are unavoidable, self selecting: no profile of the Tower could possibly be complete without a reference to the Peasants' Rebellion or the fate of Anne Boleyn – which, indeed, also illustrate vital points of change in the story of the nation. But, where possible, the less familiar has been chosen: thus, greater space has been given to John Gerard's account of being a prisoner in 1597, published in 1951, rather than the oft-told tale of the Gunpowder Plot.

An attempt has been made, too, to cover that part of the Tower's history which has been curiously overlooked in the past – its relationship, frequently prickly, with its immediate neighbour, the church and parish of All Hallows by the Tower, which was in existence at least three centuries before William the Conqueror arrived on what was to be Tower Hill.

Section I
The Fortress

As I have said, they wished to have huge buildings,
but modest expenses: to envy their equals: to surpass
their betters: to defend their subjects from outsiders
while robbing them themselves ...

William of Malmesbury on the Normans

Chapter I
In the Beginning: Londinium

London is an upstart among the cities of England.

Long before the Romans came, flourishing little communities had sprung up in areas which would become suburbs of the giant: in Barnes and Chelsea, in Fulham, Battersea, Hammersmith and Wandsworth archaeology has produced substantial evidences of prehistoric occupation. Only the central area, the 'square mile' which would give its name to the whole, remained unoccupied. There may have been active reasons for human beings to shun the spot, for the name given to this desolate scrubland was derived from the Celtic word signifying 'savage' or 'bold' or 'wild'. Whatever the reason, it was left to the Romans to create the town and they seem to have done it almost absent-mindedly, for their interests were elsewhere: at Camulodunum (Colchester) where the Emperor Claudius built the gigantic temple to his own cult which signified the unity of the Roman Empire: at Verulamium (St Albans), granted the rare privilege of self-government as a *municipium*: at the northern military capital of Eboracum (York). When the Romans left, the incoming Saxons looked south, fixing their capital, so far as they had one, at Winchester. Even as late as 1065, Edward the Confessor founded his great abbey of West Minster not in the City of London but in the marshes to the west, building a palace nearby and so creating a royal city, a second heart for the whole vast complex which would have an incalculable effect on its history.

But the City of London, with that amiable contempt for the opinion of neighbours which has characterized it throughout, just went on growing, drawing on its own vast self-generative forces.

London, of course, had one priceless asset above all other English cities: a great river road. At a time when land communication took place along narrow, rutted, muddy tracks – tracks, moreover, which could be closed down for months during the winter – an international trader could load his ship in London and comfortably, economically and with reasonable safety float it down to the Mediterranean or along the Rhine and so into the heart of Europe. 'Famed for commerce and crowded with traders', was Tacitus's view of the city, one of the rare Roman notices we have of it. Commerce was to be its lifeblood, its entire *raison d'être*, and from the beginning, down to our own time, most of that commerce came and left along the Thames. When, in the sixteenth century, an enraged Queen Mary threatened to move parliament and her court to Oxford a London alderman enquired sardonically 'whether she meant also to divert the river Thames, if not, then by God's grace we shall do well enough in London, whatsoever become of the Parliament'.

But London's power of growth had the effect of obscuring its history as succeeding generations frantically built over the traces of their predecessors. Until recently, we probably knew as little about pre-Norman London as we do about the cities of Pharoah's Egypt. And without that knowledge, the reason why William the Conqueror founded his great castle exactly where he did is also obscured. And that reason explains why the Tower of London is today no quaint ancient monument maintained for nostalgic or touristic reasons, but is still Her Majesty's Tower of London, permanently garrisoned, taut as a wound-up spring after nine centuries, a formidable fortress in the heart of the modern city.

It was the great air raids of the Second World War which began to unveil the hidden centuries. The central target of those raids was the 'City', that fabulous square mile whose boundaries still

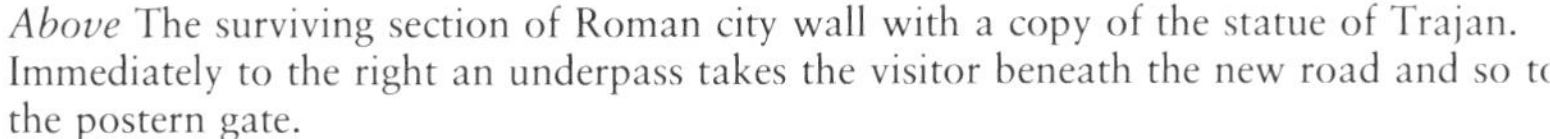

Above The surviving section of Roman city wall with a copy of the statue of Trajan. Immediately to the right an underpass takes the visitor beneath the new road and so to the postern gate.

Right above A model of Roman London, now in All Hallows's crypt. The site of Aulus Plautius's encampment, and later of the Tower, lies in the bottom right-hand corner. The permanent, Cripplegate, fort is in the top left-hand corner. The river outside the city is the Fleet, following the present line of Farringdon and New Bridge Streets.

Right below Roman mosaic pavement, discovered and *in situ* in the crypt of All Hallows Church

approximate to those of the Roman city, and its adjoining docklands which made of London the greatest port in the world. The Tower of London lies exactly at the point where dockland meets City and it suffered, as a result, more damage from enemy action than it had suffered during the previous nine hundred years of its existence. The bombardment destroyed much that was irreplaceable in London, but it also opened up much. In particular, the destroyed areas allowed a free hand for the immense development of the post-war years. A lot of the architecture which went up was, frankly, appalling, and it can only be hoped that London's digestive powers will take care of it some time in the future. But the vast new buildings required equally vast foundations, greater in area and depth than ever known before, laying bare to archaeologists evidences going back two thousand years and more.

The archaeology which opened up pre-Norman London is of the most rigorously academic type. Apart from the Temple of Mithras (itself consisting of only low foundations and some statuary small in quantity if superb in quality) there have been no dramatic discoveries. No rich burial producing grave goods to throw light on the course of a civilization: no inscribed tablets of stone to eke out the sparse evidences in manuscript. Instead, it has been the painstaking examination of layers of gravel: of the fact that clay here has been trodden hard or that a rubbish pit was dug over there, rather than over here. Pebbles found in one particular place seem a completely trivial discovery, for instance, but they show that the Thames must have been shallower, and faster flowing than in our own time, with a correspondingly important effect upon the interpretation of historic events. Putting together these seemingly ephemeral evidences, the archaeologist provides for the historian a kind of backcloth, sketching in an outline still tantalizingly vague in parts but comprehensible as a whole, of the London that William the Conqueror would have seen as he decided where to build the greatest castle in his realm.

Some twelve feet below the streets of the modern City of London there lies a layer of reddish earth roughly one foot thick. The colour is the result of great heat, calculated at around 1,000°C and was itself the result of an immense conflagration which reduced the city to ashes in the year AD60. That was the year in which the tribe of the Iceni, led by their queen Boudicca, turned upon their Roman overlords and destroyed the cities of Camulodunum, Verulamium and Londinium. The event, catastrophic to its inhabitants, is of priceless value to posterity for through it we know that a major city was in existence on the north bank of the Thames by that year. The city could not have been founded before AD43 for that was the year of the first Roman occupation and, as we have seen, no traces of any prehistoric settlement has ever been found on the site. We therefore have an unusually narrow slot of seventeen years in which to place the founding of what was to be the capital of a world empire.

Both archaeology and history give us a fairly clear idea of what happened during those spring days of AD43. The watching Britons who saw the great galleys moving up the Kent coast, their huge sweeps riding and falling in perfect synchronization so that they resembled multi-legged insects moving with ominous purpose, may well have had a tribal memory of Julius Caesar's invasion eighty years before. There would, too, have been well-polished stories brought by travellers from the Continent about the inexorable advance of the bronze-clad legions, but nothing could have prepared the Britons for what was to come. The Romans landed in Richborough, on the Kent coast, built their usual strongpoint and then began advancing north-westward. The local tribes, led by the brothers Caratacus and Togodumnus, fought back bravely, but before that irresistible bronze pressure, steadily fell back to the Thames. This southern bank of the river consisted of a half-mile-wide stretch of marshland through which a few gravelly paths made their way as natural highways. Local knowledge stood the Britons in good stead and, threading their way through the marshes, they safely crossed by a ford some considerable way upstream. The Roman army under its commander Aulus Plautius reached the southern bank and paused.

What they saw across the river was not very impressive. The site of future London consisted of two low hills, nowhere higher than about thirty feet, covered with scrub and low oak trees. The two hills were separated by a narrow, deep gulley down which flowed a little stream, the Walbrook, some fourteen feet wide. Further to the west was a much larger river, the Fleet, over a hundred yards wide at its mouth, which separated the two hillocks from the flat lands beyond. The river, broader, shallower and faster than it is today and not yet subject to tidal influence, presented a formidable barrier. Nevertheless Aulus Plautius launched a successful crossing, his German mercenaries, trained to swim in full equipment, crossing individually and occupying the point of landing while the main body crossed either by pontoon bridge or small boats.

What happened next on the site can be built up only by analogy with other Roman military campaigns and by our knowledge of what was happening in the wider world of the Roman Empire. The lame, stuttering, thoroughly unimpressive Emperor Claudius badly needed a formal 'triumph' in Rome to establish himself and he could have one only after a campaign of conquest. Britain presented one almost, if not quite, on a plate. Aulus Plautius had broken the back of resistance, there remaining now only the advance on the tribal capital of Camulodunum in the north-east and Claudius was determined to take part in that, ordering his commander to await his imperial coming. This hillock on the north bank of the Thames, defended on two sides by water, made an excellent site for a temporary encampment and here Aulus Plautius waited. Like all good commanders he would have realized that idle troops were dangerous troops and it is probable that, while waiting, he set them to work building the first London Bridge. Not even the phenomenal Roman skill at bridge-building could have produced a stone bridge in the time available and this first bridge was undoubtedly made of wood. No trace whatsoever of it survives, but its approximate locality can be calculated from the known alignment of Roman roads converging on it and the fact that its southern end would have had to make contact with one of the gravel islets in the marshes. Evidently, it lay some little way downstream of the present London Bridge, closer to the future site of the Tower of London and its position was to be the deciding factor as to whether or not a city would rise in this locality. Claudius came, probably crossing the new bridge in splendour with his elephants, advanced on Camulodunum with his victorious general, laid the foundation stone of his great temple and, after sixteen days, returned to Rome, to his Triumph and to his death at the hands of his bestial nephew. The Roman occupation of Britain had begun in earnest.

Archaeological investigations of London's city wall shows that where it passes through what is now the Tower of London it makes a curious change of direction: instead of continuing on in a straight line to the south-east it swings one or two degrees to the south-west. The most reasonable explanation of this change of direction is that the builders were economically making use of an existing stretch of wall or bank, and this would probably have been the eastern wall or bank of Aulus Plautius's encampment, giving the site of the Tower of London, as a military area, an overall history of some 1,900 years. The encampment, however, was temporary for, in founding London, the Romans departed from their normal custom. A more or less standard pattern for the foundation of cities in barbarian lands was first to create a fort and then turn that fort into a town when its military use was ended: York, Colchester, Chester, Winchester all saw this gradual transformation with the via Decumanis and the via Principalis becoming the main arteries of the new town.

Not so with London. The only military presence would have been in that small fort whose remains lie under the Tower: elsewhere the city was laid out simply as a port. So confident were the Romans of their hold on South-East England that they did not even trouble to build a wall around their new foundation, as the new-born race of Londoners found to their cost during the Boudiccan revolt when 'Romans and friends of Rome were massacred, hanged, burned and crucified'. But, remarkably, it was not until the turn of the century, at least forty years after the massacre and at least sixty years after the foundation of the city, that a permanent fort was built.

In his book summing up post-war excavations in London, the archaeologist Peter Marsden warns the reader, 'Because there is a continuing programme of excavation, there can be no final word on the subject of Roman London'. Here, at the very outset of London's history, we encounter a conundrum. Why did the Romans, those superlative military engineers, build their permanent fort in the far north-western corner of their city instead of the south-east corner where it would not only have the protection of the Thames, but also defend the vital bridge and the ceremonial buildings rising in the area? This, after all, had been the site chosen by Aulus Plautius and would be the site unhesitatingly chosen by William the Conqueror. It may be that the Romans thought that the river was defence enough, and that they had more reason to fear a land-based attack from the north than a waterborne attack by tribesmen who had not yet mastered the art of shipbuilding or navigation. Whatever the reason, it was in the area now known as Cripplegate that they built a fortress three times the size of the norm, garrisoning it with men from all three of the regular British legions, evidence of the importance of the growing city.

Overshadowing the puzzle of the siting of the fort is the puzzle of the dating of the immense circuit of the city wall. This was not built until some time around the year 200, long after Britain was firmly under Roman control and no danger could possibly come

Above A Saxon arch in All Hallows Church, built at least three centuries before the commencement of the Tower and uncovered by Second World War bombardment

Left The base of the Roman riverside wall within the Tower, discovered in 1976, flanked by the later curtain wall

from revolting tribesmen. The building of the city wall perhaps reflects the disturbance within the Empire which ended with the emergence of Septimus Severus. But the danger was deemed to be so great, and London so important that it apparently justified one of the major architectural enterprises of Roman Britain. Even today, nearly two thousand years after its construction, the Roman wall defines much of the City of London, the street system following its course even where the wall itself has disappeared. The most spectacular section is just outside the Tower of London where bomb damage allowed the wall to be cleared of the accretions of centuries. Standing on the small lawn that has been laid at its base, one can get the unique impression of actually being inside the ancient city, protected from the hostile outer world by that massive stone shield towering high in the air. Even as late as the Civil War of the seventeenth century the wall was fulfilling its function, when the exterior ditch was re-dug as a defence against the Royalists. On the western side the Fleet river created a natural moat and although wall and river have long since disappeared, Farringdon Street marks the boundary with Newgate Street, and Ludgate Hill still marks the entrances from the west. The wall, some two miles in circuit, was built of Kentish ragstone, brought in by boat. In 1961 the remains of one of these boats, still loaded with its cargo of stone, was found on the bed of the Thames where it had sunk after apparently being involved in a collision right at the end of its journey from Maidstone.

And behind that wall the Roman city took its final form, effortlessly overtaking its rivals to emerge as the undoubted capital of Britannia. Bisecting the city was the little Walbrook stream. By the Middle Ages that stream would become an open sewer so disgusting that even the hardy Londoners, accustomed to a wide range of stinks, were constrained to cover it over. But in the Roman city it was still a pure little stream along whose banks appeared luxurious villas as well as that Temple of Mithras uncovered in 1954. The ceremonial heart of Londinium lay to the east of the Walbrook: there was established the immense forum and basilica, the largest in Britain. There too was the governor's palace, stretching down to the river. The standard of comfort, and indeed of luxury was high, shown by the elaborate mosaics uncovered from time to time, the most recent being found after the Second World War bombardment in the crypt of All Hallows Church by the Tower. Nearby in Billingsgate, the earliest of London's 'ports', the ruins of a house were discovered in 1968, together with an elaborate bath house. This latter, too large for a private house but too small for a public bath house argues that the building might have been an inn for a prosperous class of trader. For the whole of this area in the south-east corner of Londinium, the area that would in time come to be known as Tower Hill, was the very heart of the 'port of London'. Traders from all over the Mediterranean brought in their goods: luxury goods for the most part – fine wines, exquisite glassware: olive oil in great amphorae: silver and bronze ware. The laden ships leaving the quay carried goods from a colonial outpost that would fetch good prices in Italy: fine wool: furs: lead: slaves: gold. It was a commercial rhythm that would rise and fall over the centuries but never entirely die away until the technological revolution of the second half of the twentieth century abruptly killed it off.

For many years there was an ongoing debate among archaeologists and historians as to whether the Romans had completed the circuit of the city wall by building along the river front. It seemed an obvious thing to do, and a twelfth-century chronicler recorded that there had been a wall but that the river 'in a long space of time undermined and subverted the walls on the south side of the City'. It was not until 1976, however, that there came uncontrovertible evidence when, during excavations at the Tower of London for the construction of the new history gallery, a section of Roman wall, built approximately during the 390s and running roughly parallel with the river, was uncovered. It was a massive construction, some twenty feet high with an internal timber facing, its line dictating the plan of all subsequent building in the area, and evidently built in haste for earth had been heaped up on the landward side before the mortar had been rendered. The size of the wall, the haste of construction and the dating all have one significance. The Roman Empire, that must have seemed all but eternal, was under attack. The cities which it had created could no longer look to it for protection and must fend for themselves. There were other indications of an end of the Golden Age: in 1777 not far from that section of wall were discovered a silver ingot and some gold coins, buried no doubt for protection after the year 395.

There was no dramatic onslaught on Roman London: no horde of yelling savages to plunder and destroy. Instead the life simply ebbed from the great city. The house in Billingsgate gives a time-scale: it was still occupied about the year 400 when a hoard of bronze coins was carefully hidden in a wall but some time about the year 450 a prowling Saxon dropped a brooch in the bath house. The guardians of the Temple of Mithras buried their sacred sculptures to protect them from Christian hands, but no Christian church solid enough to leave traces of itself was built. All over the city the great villas and palaces gradually crumbled. Squatters moved into the governor's palace, building a crude hearth against one of the beautifully painted walls. They also moved into the Billingsgate house, until the roof collapsed.

By the year 410 an almost impenetrable darkness falls on the city. The probability is that it reverted to a purely rural economy, for the wide sweep of the walls enclosed a number of market gardens and farms even in the city's heyday. But though the pulse of London beat slowly and feebly it never quite stopped and by the seventh century had begun to pick up again. Even the invading Saxons, who looked on towns as 'sepulchres for the living' could not escape the gravitational pull of England's largest town, and had actually begun to build there. All Hallows, the little church that stands on the doorstep of the Tower of London and was destined to have a somewhat prickly relationship with its mighty neighbour down the centuries, was rebuilt by the Saxons in what was, for them, a substantial manner. The great air raid of 1940, which literally opened up the church, disclosed a Saxon arch as well as Saxon tombstones. The centuries-long struggle between Saxons, Danes, Vikings during which the kingdom of England was slowly, painfully hammered into being, gradually centred around London. But throughout those long centuries, the south-east corner of the city lay empty with, perhaps, some Roman foundations a few feet below crudely tilled soil.

Unused – until the coming of the Normans.

Chapter II
The Coming of the Normans

The Norman conquest of England in the eleventh century is one of the disregarded mysteries of history. How was it that a force of less than 10,000 men, many of whom were mercenaries, managed to subdue a kingdom of, at the very least, a million people? The actual Battle of Hastings was a straightforward clash between roughly equal forces, with the Normans having the undoubted advantage of cavalry. In the weeks immediately following the battle, simple terror was an effective weapon against a stunned population: the dispassionate pages of Domesday record the catastrophic fall in property values as the Normans savaged their way through southern England. It is what happened during the following months that constitutes the puzzle. In town after town, relatively small groups of Normans – rarely numbering more than hundreds – held down a highly intelligent, resourceful and deeply resentful population of townsfolk running into thousands. Once established, however, the Normans had a supreme weapon with which to maintain their dominance: the castle. Looking back a generation later, the chronicler Odericus Vitalis was of the opinion that the Norman conquest would never have succeeded had the English possessed castles, for the invaders would have exhausted their strength in a series of sieges.

The English were by no means unfamiliar with the concept of a strongpoint. A little over a generation earlier, their great king, Alfred, had established a chain of fortified towns, called *burhs*, in the long struggle against the Danes. But the Saxon dislike of enclosed places told against them. By contrast the Normans, perhaps consciously copying those Romans whom they so closely resembled, carried the strongpoint to its logical conclusion: a place from which a minority could control a majority. William even brought over a prefabricated wooden castle with him when he landed at Pevensey and it was erected by nightfall of the same day. Immediately after the victory at Hastings, he ordered a castle to be built in the town itself, a move so important that it figured in the Bayeux tapestry. Here, very clearly, is shown the Norman technique of motte and bailey which enabled them to hold all England in an iron grip. Working with crude shovels, labourers – almost certainly Saxon slaves – are heaping up a mound, the motte, which is already crowned by its keep. Not the least of Norman skills was their ability to place a massive keep on a recently created mound.

From Hastings, the Norman castle-builders moved on to Dover, utilizing there the existing Roman foundations, then on to Canterbury where again, the Conqueror 'built a tower'. So, advancing always from a secure base, William moved on to London.

The Battle of Hastings was fought on 14 October: the Saxon thanes eventually acknowledged William as overlord at Berkhamstead in Berkshire in mid-December. During those weeks, William prowled around London like a wolf seeking entry. Only once since the Boudiccan massacre had the city fallen to attack and that second occasion had been waterborne, the attackers forcing an entry through the presumably crumbling river wall. Elsewhere the great Roman walls defied an army without siege equipment and William had no choice but to wait for a political solution. When it came he reacted immediately, a detachment of engineers being hurriedly despatched from Berkhampstead to London to build a temporary castle. William himself stayed in London only long enough for his coronation in Westminster on Christmas Day, then prudently withdrew to Barking, a mile or so to the east of the city 'while certain fortifications were completed in the city against the fickleness of the vast and fierce populace'.

Above The White Tower, showing the thickness of the walls; the window is a post-Norman insertion

Right A passage within the thickness of the White Tower's walls

Opposite For at least a century, from 1100 to 1200, the White Tower was the only major building. Originally so called because it was whitewashed in the reign of Henry III, it still gleams in sunlight. The wall in the foreground is the Main Guard, built *c*1230 as an inner curtain wall and uncovered by the aerial bombardment of the Second World War.

The engineers built not one, but three castles: in the south-east corner of the city on the site of the long-vanished Roman encampment, and two others further to the west along the river front. These, later known as Baynard's and Mountfichet castle, have long since disappeared but the building in the south-east corner was destined to evolve into the Tower. Excavations in 1964 prove what commonsense deduces, that the first 'castle' in London, like the other castles raised during the campaign, was a hastily built complex of raised earth walls topped with a wooden palisade. The builders had the inestimable advantage of the Roman city wall on the eastern side and the river and, probably, the remains of the Roman river wall on the south. A trench or ditch was dug westward from the wall, then curving south towards the river, ending at the site of the later Bloody Tower. The southern section of this ditch was excavated in 1975 and left uncovered so that it is possible to see today evidence of work that must have been carried on at great speed and under conditions of considerable tension, as the chronicler testifies with his reference to 'the fickleness of the vast and fierce mob'. Some time during the next decade, the foundations of the White Tower were laid within this crude enclosure.

The dating of this, the first of all stone keeps in England and, with the exception of Colchester, the largest, can only be approximate. Its architect, Gundulf, is referred to as Bishop of Rochester and he did not become Bishop until 1077. The implication, therefore, is that the keep was not commenced until some ten years after the Conquest. Work upon it, however, was far advanced by the time of William's death in 1087 and it was certainly completed before the end of the century. It was not surprising that William chose a churchman for his architect for, during the tremendous phase of monastic and church building that characterized France in the opening of the eleventh century, bishops and abbots necessarily gained wide experience of building on a large scale. Gundulf had been a monk first of the abbey of Bec, then at Caen under its Abbot Lanfranc who later became the first Norman Archbishop of Canterbury and the builder of its cathedral. Gundulf followed suit, rebuilding his own cathedral at Rochester as well as supervising work at the Tower, earning the contemporary tribute that he was 'very competent and skilful at building in stone'.

The White Tower entered history with a sinister legend, for it was widely believed that dragon's blood had been mixed with the mortar. The reddish tinge, in fact, was produced by the crushed Roman brick that was used, but the rumour was testimony to the fear and hatred created by the vast building, so huge that it would give its name to the whole complex so that history knows it as the Tower, not the Castle, of London.

Considering that it has been continuously occupied for nearly nine centuries, the White Tower is curiously little changed, all later exterior accretions having been demolished by the nineteenth century. Most of the windows were altered in the eighteenth century and, inside, an additional floor was inserted reducing the height, and so the impact, of what was the king's great chamber on the second floor. The Tower's modern use as a musem of arms and armour also rather obscures its original form and function. But the visitor still ascends from one floor to another by the tightly winding spiral staircase set in the thickness of the wall and known technically as a 'vice', and the majestic chapel is the only one in Britain today – and one of the very few Norman chapels in all Europe – to look today exactly as it did when the builders' scaffolding was taken down.

Gundulf's design for the White Tower was innovative, reflecting the embattled state of Europe. No longer was it possible, as it had been during the Roman and Carolingian Empires, for the many buildings of a palace – its hall, its chapel, its many service rooms – to be scattered around. All functions had to be withdrawn behind a stone shield. Gundulf's Tower was actually referred to as an *arx palatina*, a fortress palace, where a powerful man might find safety together with what comforts were available in a brutal age. Norman castles never became as rigidly standardized as the Roman fort but the main details of the White Tower were to appear again and again in the dozens of castles that were beginning to rise above the towns of England. The entrance was on the first floor by means of an easily defended wooden staircase. The basement, extending over the whole area, was given over to stores which, together with the well, ensured that the keep could hold out for the longest siege. The first floor with its latrines set in the wall (known as *garderobes*) and its fireplaces was the residential area for the less important members of the household. The second floor was the ceremonial area: here the king sat in state to receive emissaries or pronounce judgements: here he banqueted: here he slept. As with all Norman keeps of the period there appears to be no permanent provision for sleeping quarters. The great room, like the two below, was divided by a wall running approximately down the centre, but that is the only permanent structure and unless there was a number of smaller wooden structures the household would simply have slept wherever it could, and certainly without privacy apart from that provided by the latrines in the wall. Curiously, there is no fireplace as on the floor below so presumably there must have been a central hearth. Eight of the original windows survive on this floor from which one can get a clear idea of the general level of lighting: given their relative small size, it must have been poor. Originally, this room rose high to the roof with a gallery running inside the wall halfway up, and immediately adjoining it is the chapel. Whether it was the ecclesiastical influence of Gundulf, or the result of William's own very real piety, this chapel of St John was deemed so important that, though small, it actually projects out from the main body of the building in the form of an apse, its lower portions forming two crypts, one above the other, which were to have very different functions in the ensuing centuries. And here, in the chapel, one comes the closest it is possible to come to the Norman spirit, that powerful, utterly ruthless driving force which led a small nation to put its imprint on a continent. The massive strength of the chapel is due partly to the fact that the masons had not yet discovered that secret of the pointed arch which would later allow them to impart lightness to the towering cathedrals and churches. But its solemn grandeur is due to the instinct for architectural beauty possessed by these former Norsemen.

The year 1097 was a terrible year for the English, the *Anglo-Saxon Chronicle* noted: bad weather, ruined harvests and 'unjust taxes that never ceased'. Worse was to come. 'Many shires, who were on service with work in London, were sorely oppressed because of the wall on which they worked around the Tower, and the bridge which was nearly all broken up by the flood, and through the work on the king's hall at Westminster.' Arguably, the work on London Bridge was for the good of all, but the forced labour brought in for the other two projects was for the aggrandizement of a hated foreign overlord. The king now was William Rufus, as harsh and overbearing as his father, settling the 'Norman yoke' more firmly round the necks of the English until his mysterious death in the New Forest. His hall at Westminster (now part of the Houses of Parliament) took two years to build and was one of the largest in Europe. Its creation gave yet more status to West Minster as the seat of royalty: certainly William preferred to live there rather than at the Tower. Nevertheless, the building of the wall described by the *Anglo-Saxon Chronicle* showed that he had every intention of carrying on his father's work at the great castle which held down the city of London. The wall followed the line of ditch and palisade but, built of stone, greatly increased the possibilities of defence.

By the year 1100, therefore, the Tower of London consisted of the immense, ninety-foot-high keep crammed rather uneasily in the upper half of an enclosure that was not much wider than itself. The lower, southern half near the river was the bailey, not much larger than the floor area of the keep itself, as with other baileys used partly as a parade ground and for such services as stabling, armouries and the like. Most of the ordinary, day-to-day life of the garrison would have been carried on in this decidedly restricted area and, remarkably, no further attempt to enlarge the area would be undertaken for at least another century. We can get quite a good idea of what the complex looked like by comparing it with Portchester castle as it looks today. There the Roman walls of the original fort are still intact with the Norman keep towering above them although, unlike the White Tower, it actually abuts the walls.

The Saxon labourers could scarcely have finished work upon the curtain wall when the Tower of London received the first of the hundreds of prisoners who would languish in it over the centuries. But 'languish' is perhaps not quite the word for the imprisonment of Ranulf Flambard, Bishop of Durham and one-time Justiciar for William II. Flambard possessed to the full that rapacity which marked all Norman dealings with the people they conquered, and exercised it unchecked for he was exercising it on behalf of his master. The fact that much of the gold he squeezed out of William's unfortunate subjects stuck to his fingers went unremarked for he had the good sense to ensure that William's coffers were kept replenished. But the hatred he earned made him a target the moment that death removed his protector. The new, energetic, young king, Henry I, promptly threw Flambard into the Tower – where he landed very comfortably indeed.

The Tower's reputation as a grisly torture chamber rose largely as a result of the religious struggles of the sixteenth century, the legends fanned by such lurid propaganda works as Foxe's *Book of Martyrs*. In the main, those detained in the Tower were deprived of their liberty only and were not only permitted, but expected, to make themselves as comfortable as their resources allowed. There were no dungeons, as such, prisoners being lodged wherever was convenient. These two factors contributed directly to Flambard's escape – for Flambard achieved two firsts, the first of many to be

imprisoned but the first of many, too, to depart unofficially. He was lodged in the banqueting hall of the White Tower, living literally like a lord for six months, served by his personal servants and in regular contact with the outside world. In the late afternoon of 2 February 1101, he gave a banquet for his guards – a banquet where wine flowed very generously indeed. Later that night, with the guards presumably quite comatose, he lowered a rope from a window, slipped down it, somehow got over the new encircling wall and was away.

Flambard had been housed in the White Tower for there was no other accommodation within the castle, the buildings in the bailey almost certainly consisting only of temporary hutments, unfit for a prisoner of Flambard's status and certainly unfit for the king. This was another factor which contributed to the Justiciar's escape, for if the king had been in residence no guard would have dreamed of carousing with a prisoner under the fierce eye of young King Henry. It was not until the disastrous reign of Stephen, who came to the throne in 1135, that a permanent residence for the monarch was built in the bailey, the beginnings of the palace that would develop there over the next four centuries until Henry VIII took up residence in White Hall, the royal city of West Minster exerting its final, successful pull over the commercial City of London. Stephen's palace must have been claustrophobically cramped, for it was still hemmed in by the towering Roman city wall on one side and the river wall on the south, but it provided safety in a murderous period when 'Men said openly that Christ and his saints slept'.

Stephen's character provides a textbook example of the fact that a 'good' monarch is a strong monarch, regardless of morals. He was popular enough, but a chronicler dismissed him devastatingly as 'A mild man, soft and good – and did no justice', the worst possible kind of monarch to reign when the succession was in dispute. Henry had made his barons swear to recognize his daughter Matilda as his heir, but as soon as he was dead support switched to her cousin Stephen, the English disliking the idea of a woman as monarch – and scenting, too, the advantages to be wrung from a weak king. For eight years the civil war raged, the

The White Tower: the chapel of St John, a perfect example of Norman ecclesiastical architecture, still used for church services

The line of the Roman city wall within the Tower – note how close the White Tower is to the wall. The low ruins straddling the line of the wall are the remains of the Wardrobe Tower.

barons switching from one side to another as advantage offered. This was the great age of castle building, 'stone spurs' in a chronicler's vivid phrase, 'which disembowelled the king', each the centre of a little state whence the local baron could defy the rest of the world. 'Every great man built him castles and held them against the king and they filled the whole land with these castles. They sorely burdened the unhappy people of the country with forced labour on the castles, and when the castles were built they filled them with devils and wicked men.' And in the chaos the Tower changed hands again and again for the Constable, who supposedly held it for the king, shared the general ethos and placed his loyalty where the purse was the fullest.

The office of Constable of the Tower of London ranks among the oldest in the world for the first was appointed, by William the Conqueror himself, in 1078 when the White Tower was only a few feet high, and the last was appointed, by Elizabeth II in 1985, the only break occurring in the reign of Elizabeth I when, for some reason, no Constables are recorded. Today a purely honorary office, in the early centuries of the castle's history it was utterly vital, as Stephen found to his cost.

His Constable, Geoffrey de Mandeville, was the son and grandson of previous Constables and evidently regarded his office as safely hereditary. A stronger king would have rapidly disabused him of the idea but Stephen was simply a pawn. In 1141 Stephen was actually captured by Matilda's forces whereupon de Mandeville promptly 'sold' her the Tower in exchange for an earldom and other lucrative offices. Matilda queened it briefly in London until driven out by the enraged Londoners, exasperated by her arrogance. De Mandeville, now boasting the title of earl of Essex made his second switch, imprisoning Matilda's supporter, the Bishop of London, and pledging 'loyalty' to Stephen in exchange for yet more lands and honours. Yet again, Stephen accepted his Constable's now thoroughly tarnished sword and it was only when de Mandeville was discovered, yet again, in communication with Matilda that Stephen summoned up his courage to dismiss him from office. The writer of the *Life of Stephen* employs a vivid phrase which sums up the character of the late Constable: he left the royal audience 'like a vicious and riderless horse, kicking and biting in his rage'. Stephen evidently did not dare to imprison him and de Mandeville departed to set up trade as an outlaw in East Anglia until his inevitable death by violence.

Never again did the vital office of Constable descend almost as of right from father to son, thereafter the king carefully choosing the magnate he could trust: thus Henry II appointed his close friend and confidant, Thomas à Becket, to the office and though he occupied it only a year or so before being appointed Archbishop of Canterbury he too took part in the gradual expansion of the royal palace within the walls. But the position was by no means a sinecure. The Constable's responsibilities extended far beyond the walls of the Tower: he was also responsible to the king for the City of London itself, dealing with prickly, stiff-necked citizens whom the courtly French chronicler, Jean Froissart, regarded with horror. 'The English are the worst people in the world, the most obstinate and presumptuous. And of all the English the Londoners are the leaders for, to say the truth, they are very powerful in men and wealth.' Dealing with them, the Constable had to tread his way through a species of minefield. Not the least onerous and delicate of his duties was his guardianship of the Jews from the attacks by Christians. One of the few activities which a Jew could legally undertake was moneylending: a Christian debtor could happily combine religious prejudice with financial gain by eliminating the Jew and, with him, the debt. Again and again, the Jewish community came under savage attack. At the coronation of Richard I in 1189, leaders of the Jewish community rather touchingly – and, in the event, unwisely – entered Westminster Hall with rich gifts for the new king. Enraged by the 'sacrilege', the mob murdered some of the leaders and then invaded the Jewry, the area near Cheapside to which Jews were confined, and put it to the torch. There undoubtedly would have been an horrific general massacre, along the lines of the massacre at York, if the Tower had not opened its gates to the terrified people. At the next coronation, that of Henry III, the entire London Jewish community numbering some one thousand people took refuge in the Tower before the ceremonies began. Actual maintenance of order in the Jewry was the responsibility of one of the Constable's officers, the Serjeant of the Jewry, who had the power of expelling Christians from the ghetto. None of these measures was due to altruism: the Jews were a sort of royal milch-cow, specifically and legally the 'property' of the king who from time to time would squeeze the community dry of gold under pretext of fine or taxation, until their total expulsion from the kingdom in 1290.

For over a century, ever since the commencement of the White Tower, the City of London had been living in uneasy proximity to its mighty neighbour, here resisting where possible any further encroachment on its liberties, there nibbling away at the royal power as represented by the Constable. In the 1190s chance gave them an excellent bargaining power when William Longchamp, Bishop of Ely and Constable of the Tower, was urgently trying to scrape money together for his royal master, Richard Coeur de Lion. Legend has cast the blond, handsome King Richard into the role of hero, with his sly, stunted brother John as villain, but it is debatable as to which did more damage to their country, Richard as an absentee landlord endlessly demanding money for his preposterous crusades (he spent just five months of his ten-year reign in England) or John with his maniacal rages and almost pathological ambition. Almost as though deliberately creating a conflict Richard delegated power not to his brother who, though hated, was at least of royal stock, but to an equally hated man of base origins, for Longchamp was descended from a French serf:

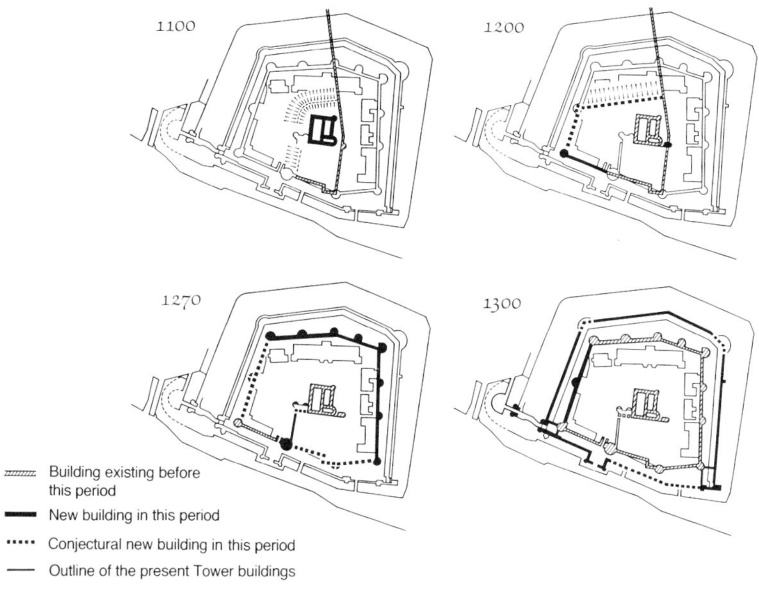

The main stages in the development of the Tower

'The laity found him more than king, the clergy more than Pope, and both an intolerable tyrant'. John openly set up an administration opposing Longchamp, those who saw profit in strife flocked to him – and so triggered off the next great wave of building at the Tower. A clash was inevitable, and Longchamp hastened not only to strengthen but to expand his power base.

Apart from the building of the western wall nearly a century earlier, there had been little change. Longchamp now more than doubled the area enclosing the keep by extending the southern or river wall westward, and then built the first of the great towers of the encircling wall, the massive bastion at the corner which would be known as the Bell Tower. He also, for the first time, actually encroached upon the Roman city wall which ran a few yards to the east of the keep, building a tower upon it called the Wardrobe Tower and linking it to the keep. A new ditch was dug outside the new western wall and there were even ambitious plans to link it to the Thames but this came to nothing for the planned moat simply emptied itself at low tide. All this not only cost a great deal of money, but also annoyed the neighbours, for the City of London objected strongly to the new encroachments and, as John and Longchamp manoeuvred for position, London was in a position to make its displeasure known. In exchange for a cash payment, Longchamp ceded his right of 'tax farming' the city: thereafter, London would levy its own taxes – and decide what to do with them. More, they even gained the right to elect their own sheriffs and finally, for the first time, achieved a corporate identity in the form of the first Mayor of the City of London.

The concessions did Longchamp little good, for the Londoners, deciding that they preferred the native to the foreign devil, joined forces with John and besieged the Tower. Longchamp appeared to have little faith in his own defences and, within three days, this first siege of the Tower was at an end, Longchamp first surrendering to John and then escaping to France. From then on John, king of England, was free to pursue a lunatic career which led to Runnymede and his enforced signing of Magna Carta and, even more bizarrely, to the spectacle of the Dauphin of France enthroned in the Tower of London as a potential monarch, a lever the barons were quite prepared to use to rid the kingdom of a king who seemed barely sane. Death resolved the problem for them, removing John at the age of forty-eight, Louis the Dauphin was persuaded to depart and John's nine-year-old son Henry emerged as King Henry III.

Chapter III
The Splendid Palace

At the coronation of the boy king, a simple circlet of gold had to be used in place of the state crown which had been lost, by his father John, in a disastrous crossing of the Wash in Norfolk – an involuntary symbol of the chaos that Henry inherited. He was to remain on the throne for fifty-six years, a length of sovereignty surpassed only by George III in the eighteenth century and Victoria in the nineteenth. During that period, the Tower was to emerge almost into its final form even while the kingdom of England took one great step towards parliamentary government.

Henry liked to boast that he was the first true English king for, unlike his predecessors since the Conquest, he was actually born in England, in Winchester. Nevertheless, all his instincts were French and he married a French princess, Eleanor of Provence, to whom he was devoted throughout their long marriage. '*La Belle*' she was called because of her beauty and she brought with her not only the culture of Provence but also a depthless extravagance, two characteristics which Henry shared for he too was an aesthete and regarded money simply as a conduit of culture.

They were married in 1236 when Henry was twenty-nine and Eleanor just fourteen and the enchanted bridegroom determined to mark the occasion with a true coronation, unlike that hurried ceremony of his childhood. London would long remember the spectacular procession when Henry and his bride went from the Tower to Westminster Abbey – the Abbey he himself had rebuilt – and so unconsciously inaugurated the custom of the monarch proceeding from the Tower, through the City and so to the Abbey which was to continue down to the time of Charles II. The Londoners were delighted, sweeping their filthy streets, hanging out tapestries, cheering madly: within a few years they were to have a somewhat different view of the Provençal influence.

Inaugurated by Henry III in 1236, the ceremony of the coronation procession from the Tower to Westminster carried on until the coronation of Charles II. This is the procession of the boy king Edward VI (son of Henry VIII) in 1547.

Work had begun on the Tower when he was still a minor, his guardians intent upon providing a safe power base for the monarchy during a period of frantic political and social upheaval. It was exactly the kind of grandiose concept which would appeal to Henry's extravagant but fastidious nature and, as soon as he was of age to make his own decisions, he threw himself wholeheartedly into making the Tower of London a place of beauty as well as strength. For at least fifty years the locality must have resounded endlessly to the chink of masons' chisels: for fifty years barges laden with ragstone from Kent, with Portland stone from the southern coast, with Caen stone from France made their way to the still makeshift wharf adapted from the old Roman waterfront. The most dramatic change was the breaching of the Roman city wall for the first time. For over a thousand years the wall had loomed over the complex, much patched but still the legacy of Rome, dwarfed only by the White Tower. Now it disappeared in its entirety where it bounded the castle complex and a new length of wall appeared some fifty yards eastward of its line. Nine of the nineteen great mural towers, each of them a small castle in its own right, were built during Henry's reign, not only improving defence, but vastly increasing residential areas and each would develop a characteristic of its own. In the west, the remorselessly advancing walls engulfed the little parish church of St Peter ad Vincula, to the indignation of the Londoners. They were delighted when the massive landgate built in the western wall collapsed under its own weight and tales were told of how that great Londoner, St Thomas à Becket, had been seen striking the wall and gate with his crozier, indignant, too, about the encroachment on his beloved city. The more prosaic explanation is that the wall was built over the newly filled ditch that had been excavated by Longchamp in the previous reign and the engineers in due course overcame the problem. Henry, too, encircled his new walls with a water-filled moat, but had the good sense to go to a Flemish hydraulic engineer to advise on the building of the sluices. By about the middle of his reign the Tower of London was a most formidable complex, the White Tower still dominating all but now rather the first among equals than a unique structure, girded round by massive walls which, in their turn, stood behind a water-filled moat which was no longer affected by the capricious effect of the tides.

But it was not only masons and carpenters and engineers who were attracted to this permanent building site: there were artists, too, from Provence and Italy summoned by the artistic king Henry to turn a fortress into a palace. The two chapels received his particular attention. The modest little ex-parish church of St Peter's was transformed under his personal attention. 'The little Mary with her tabernacle and the figure of St Peter, St Nicholas and St Catherine to be newly coloured, all with the best colours . . . two fair cherubim with cheerful and pleasant countenances to be placed on either side of the great crucifix... .' The austere grandeur of the chapel of St John was softened by a mass of rich furnishings and ornaments. The great keep itself was whitewashed, giving it at last the name of the White Tower with which it would go down in history.

But it was the palace proper which occupied Henry's attention. This complex of buildings, in which some of the most dramatic events of English history took place, was totally demolished in the seventeenth century. Tantalizingly, documentary records for Henry's

Opposite Henry III: building at the Tower went on throughout his long reign, as he transformed a castle into a palace

The Traitors' Gate (St Thomas's Tower), built in the 1290s; here landed such 'traitors' as Anne Boleyn and Queen Elizabeth I

work are sparse and graphic records non-existent. The famous plan of the Tower (see frontispiece) executed by Haiward and Gascoyne over three hundred years after Henry's reign, in 1597, does give some indication of the layout of the palace within the Tower although it was by then much decayed. There was, in effect, an inner enclosure whose entrance was through a massive gateway, the Coldharbour Gate, which actually adjoined the White Tower at its south-western corner. Within the enclosure were buildings for all the functions of a civilized life which, finally, relegated the White Tower to the role of storehouse, garrison and refuge only during times of extreme danger. There was the usual Great Hall: kitchens and sculleries: lavatories considerably more pleasing than the stone boxes in the keep: King's Chamber: Queen's Chamber: Great Wardrobe Chamber. From the Coldharbour Gate, a wall ran south to the greatest of all Henry's innovations, the Wakefield Tower.

Physically, the Wakefield Tower is dominated by the White Tower and, romantically, by the now legendary Bloody Tower which adjoins it. At that time, however, the Bloody Tower was simply a single-storey watergate, similar in design and function to the so-called Traitors' Gate which took over its function when Henry's son, Edward I, made the last and greatest expansion of the encircling walls. The Wakefield Tower was Henry's personal donjon or keep, the key and centrepiece of his palace – and, indeed, the only part of the palace to survive into our own time. So many and varied were the subsequent uses to which the massive and beautiful building was put – including acting as a strongroom for the Crown Jewels – that, until recently, it was all but impossible to see its original interior design. In 1967, however, the Crown Jewels were removed to their present location under the Waterloo block and the opportunity was then taken to restore the tower to something like its original grandeur. Originally, access to the tower could only be made from the palace complex, or from Henry III's private watergate, visible today as a blocked-up doorway to the right of the tower. The modern entrance takes the visitor into a massive and majestic chamber whose proportions are again visible for the first time in some seven hundred years. This was the guardroom, immediately overlooking the river, the southern wall furnished with arrow slits. Modern stairs lead up to the first floor – and to a brilliant recent example of historical reconstruction. Dominating the room is the king's chair, a plain, solid, oaken seat with the cloth of state above and behind it adding a splash of colour. On the south wall is a little oratory or private chapel – where a successor of Henry was to be murdered: in the recess are still visible the piscina, where the Mass vessels were washed, and the sedilla or seat for the officiating priest. In wintertime a bright fire burns in the immense fireplace with its hood and winter and summer alike the room is flooded with light from the great windows. It is a place in which to linger and reflect upon the immense advance of civilization illustrated by the contrast between this chamber, at once dignified and gay, with the cold, harsh, brooding interior of the White Tower.

Apart from his extensive building activities, Henry made two innovations: he established a menagerie and a Wardrobe. In 1255 the king of France made him one of those curious gifts with which kings tended to embarrass each other – an immense African elephant. It caused great interest: the chronicler Matthew Paris made a drawing of the creature, evidently done from life for it is remarkably accurate, and drew its keeper, Henricus de Flor, under its head to illustrate its size. Henry ordered an elephant house to be built – for which the city of London was obliged to pay – and over the following years more creatures were added to what was to become, centuries hence, the London Zoo. One of its occupants was a Norwegian bear which was supplied with a long chain so that it could wander down to the foreshore and fish in the river.

The Wardrobe was to be a far more significant innovation. The Wardrobe Tower, built on the site of a Roman bastion of the city wall, was in existence at the beginning of Henry's reign, and though now in ruins is thus the oldest of all the towers, the White Tower alone excepting. Originally, the Wardrobe was simply a strongroom where the king's personal effects were kept. This included not only costume and personal ornaments but the gold and silver plate which constituted a very large part of the monarchy's portable wealth. To these, Henry added, for the first time, some items of the regalia. They were still scattered around London: the major alternative repository was in Westminster Abbey and later the Jewel House in the Palace of Westminster but gradually more and more were brought to the Tower, beginning a connection which would continue up to our own time. Henry's innovation was to turn the Wardrobe into an entire department entrusted with the financing both of his household and of his armies, again beginning an association, between Tower and the military, known as Ordnance, which was to continue on down the centuries.

It is a curiosity of the Tower of London that, although it is physically one of the strongest castles in Europe, theoretically militarily impregnable, again and again it failed in its primary purpose of providing a refuge – illustrating the fact that the strongest castle is only as strong as the will of its defenders. Despite Henry's massive new fortifications, he was obliged to cede the Tower to the barons, led by Simon de Montfort, at a crucial period, altering the course of English history when he was forced to recognize that first parliament created by Montfort. And despite the enormous circumvallation that his son, Edward I, created for the Tower, in effect girding it round with a stone armour impervious to the most powerful siege engines of the day, it failed Richard II in the fourteenth century. Its very strength, perhaps, may have contributed to his downfall, creating in him a false sense of security.

Richard's reign began in splendour. He was another boy king, just nine years old at his accession in 1377. His coronation procession from the Tower to Westminster was the most spectacular yet, with an immense retinue of knights and Richard himself, fair-haired, 'as beautiful as an angel', riding a pure white horse. The Londoners, as usual, were wild with enthusiasm, welcoming a fresh start for a country only just recovering from the Black Death and drained by the Hundred Years War. But the honeymoon period was, also as usual, rapidly over, accelerated by the fact that England was virtually governed by a regency under Richard's uncle, John of Gaunt. Taxes were increased again and again to finance the disastrous war in France, and to the ordinary discontent of peasants being forced to yield yet more to a distant government for an incomprehensible purpose was added the potent ingredient of religious dissent, religious sanctioning of violence. 'When Adam delved and Eve span, who was then the gentleman?' the renegade priest John Ball proclaimed and though he was thrown into goal, others were ready to take up the challenge to authority. In Kent, they were led by Wat Tyler. Given that it is the victors who write history, it is difficult to get a clear picture of this man – drunken bully or courageous leader? There is no denying that he was an organizer of skill, lending credence to the belief that he had served as a soldier in France, for under him a mob of several thousand men were marshalled into an army and began to march on London. Simultaneously, another great mass of men began to march south from Essex. At this stage, Tyler was still recognizing – or claiming to recognize – the sanctity of the anointed king. It was the evil advisers around him whom they wished to remove, in particular John of Gaunt, the Treasurer Robert Hales and Richard's Chancellor, Simon of Sudbury, Archbishop of Canterbury.

The Men of Kent reached Blackheath, a mile or so downriver from the Tower on the south bank, on 12 June while their Essex allies moved towards the city gate of Aldgate. From Blackheath, a messenger was sent to the Tower, demanding the king's presence

to hear their grievances. Richard was then barely fourteen years of age but, despite the objections of his terror-stricken councillors, he insisted on making the journey downriver, accompanied by three nobles – the earls of Salisbury, Warwick and Suffolk – and bodyguard. At Greenwich, however, the party seems to have realized for the first time the hornet's nest that had been stirred up: both banks of the river were black with thousands of armed men who, on sight of the royal barge in midriver, put up an unholy din. On the barge, somebody's nerve broke and Richard was persuaded to turn back. There was a yell of rage from the rebels but even at this stage they seem to have been under control for the formidable bowmen among them could have killed every man in the barge. From then on, however, matters accelerated to disaster. The ordinary citizens of London, as oppressed by taxation as their rural comrades, were firmly on the rebels' side: the great gate of Aldgate was opened for the men from Essex while the drawbridge, whose raising severed London Bridge, was lowered, and the Men of Kent poured across. Their first target was the palace of the hated John of Gaunt, the splendid riverside mansion called the Savoy, on what is now the Strand, about a mile outside the city wall. This was thoroughly sacked, the furniture hacked to pieces and the place put to the torch. Drunk now with wine and success, the rebels roared through the city and soon the mansions of most of the nobility were blazing.

Late that night, young King Richard climbed to one of the turrets of the White Tower and gazed out at his capital city. Immediately below in the open space of Tower Hill and St Katherine's Hill to the east, the rebels were camped in a dense mass. In the distance could be seen the fires and the billowing smoke rising from the burning mansions. On the river, boats manned by drunken crews patrolled to ensure that no one escaped.

Right above The basement of the Wakefield Tower. The arrow slits allowed archers to command the river, which originally washed right up to the tower.

Right below The base of the Wakefield Tower from the east. The narrow entrance partly masked by the railings was the king's private watergate entrance into the tower.

Opposite The round Wakefield Tower, the principal tower after the White Tower. Immediately adjoining the palace (now covered by the green area), the Wakefield Tower also discharged the function of royal audience chamber. The adjacent Bloody Tower was the original watergate of the castle before the fourteenth-century extension.

Once again, the Tower of London had been transformed from refuge to prison for its luckless occupants. Throughout the short summer's night, king and councillors were in anxious debate. The wisest move, perhaps, would have been to sit out the siege, for the Tower would certainly not fall to a direct assault and the rebels, despite Wat Tyler's generalship, were simply a mob without discipline which, sooner or later, would have dispersed. Instead, it was decided that Richard should go to Mile End, to the east of the city, and try to reason with the insurgents. It says much for his courage, and the irresponsibility of his advisers, that this was agreed upon.

It is unclear what happened after Richard's departure. A considerable number of the rebels trailed off to Mile End but several hundred stayed milling around the Tower, eventually gaining entrance – probably through the connivance of the garrison. They roared through the apartments of the palace, sacking the king's bedroom, insulting though not otherwise harming his mother. They found their quarry, the king's closest advisers, in St John's Chapel. Presumably, these councillors had hoped that the rebels' hands would be stayed by the sacred nature of the place but Simon of Sudbury had taken the precaution of shriving his fellow councillors beforehand. It was a wise decision for the mob paid not the least attention to the idea of sanctuary: instead, Simon of Sudbury and his companions were dragged out to their deaths on Tower Hill, the first executions to take place there.

The murder of Archbishop Sudbury and his companions did not take place in St John's Chapel, as shown in this illustration from Froissart's *Chronicles*, but on Tower Hill – the first executions to take place there

Archbishop Sudbury was the first to suffer, horribly so, at the hands of a bungling executioner who was evidently called out of the mob to do the job. A log of wood was drawn up to act as a block and: 'after forgiveness granted to the executioner that should behead him, [Sudbury] kneeling down, he offered his neck to him that should smite off his head. Being stricken in the neck, but not deadly, he putting his hand to his neck said – "Aha, it is the Hand of God". He had not removed his hand from the place where the pain was, but that being suddenly stricken again, his finger ends being cut off and part of the arteries, but yet he died not, till being mangled with eight several strokes in the neck and head, he fulfilled most worthy martyrdom. His body lay unburied all that day till afternoon, none daring to give it sepulture. His head those wicked villains took and, nailing thereon his hood, and set it on London Bridge'. His companions, having witnessed this butchery, presumably endured the same process but how they met their deaths, and where the corpses of these first victims of Tower Hill were buried, no one troubled to record. The probability is that they were buried in the little church of All Hallows for, at this period, the chapel of St Peter ad Vincula within the Tower itself would still have been a simple parish church and not the charnel house it was destined to become.

It was on the following day that there occurred one of the great set pieces of English history when the boy king Richard, by sheer force of character, triumphed over the insurgents. He, and his entourage, had returned from Mile End to learn of the horror that had been perpetrated and, again, it says much for his courage that he agreed to meet Wat Tyler at Smithfield, little more than a bowshot from the Tower itself. Tyler, by now, had gone through the usual metamorphosis of the rebel. Probably drunken, confident in the knowledge of hundreds of armed men behind him, he swaggered to the meeting contemptuously addressing the youth whom his contemporaries regarded as an emissary or representative of the Creator – a man like themselves in outward form but surrounded with a supernatural aura. The Mayor of London, Sir William Walworth, who was part of the king's small group, bitterly reproached Tyler for his foul language. Tyler replied in kind: one of the two men reached for a weapon and fighting broke out between the two groups of representatives during which Walworth mortally wounded Tyler. The rebel just had strength to turn his horse about to return to his own people, but collapsed and fell to the ground between the rebel army and the king's group.

For a few seconds, the fate of England hung in the balance. Tyler's men were armed with that simple, but deadly peasant's weapon, the longbow which, at Crécy thirty-five years earlier, had brought the steel-clad chivalry of France crashing to defeat. Enraged by the loss of their leader, they could have wiped out the entire royal party with a single volley. But there was no one to give the order and in those few critical seconds while the bowmen uncertainly pulled back the cords, but did not lift the bows, Richard took charge of the situation. Riding forward, he appealed to the mob as their anointed monarch. 'Sirs, will you shoot your king? I am your captain. Let me be your leader. Let him who loves me follow me'. Then, with quite remarkable courage, he turned his back upon the mass of men and unconcernedly began to ride away. They followed him as docilely as the children of Hamelin followed the Pied Piper and in due course were dispersed, their ringleaders dealt with in the customary manner by rope and block.

And that, at the age of fourteen, was the high point of the career of Richard of Bordeaux, even though he was to reign for twenty-two years before being deposed by his cousin Henry Bolingbroke. For Richard, on a national scale and over two decades, passed through the same metamorphosis as Tyler passed within days and on the small stage of Smithfield, turning from hero to tyrant under the spur of seemingly absolute power. Shakespeare dramatized Richard's end – incidentally giving another myth to history about the Tower's origins when he makes Richard's wife, Queen Isabel say, 'This way the King will come. This is the way to Julius Caesar's ill-erected Tower, to whose flint bosom my condemned Lord is doomed prisoner by proud Bolingbroke'.

The act of abdication undoubtedly took place in the Tower, in September 1399, with Richard formally handing over the crown of England to the new king, Henry IV. Shakespeare places some highly charged speeches in Richard's mouth, as when he looks round after his abdication:

> Mine eyes are full of tears, I cannot see
> And yet salt water blinds them not so much
> But they can see a sort of traitors here

Nevertheless, he seems to have been detached enough and calm enough to act as witness in the curious Ceremony of the Bath which marked the opening of the new reign. The ceremony, which

Richard II abdicates in favour of his cousin Henry Bolingbroke (later Henry IV)

Above The reconstruction of the king's chair of state with its ceremonial canopy

Left The audience chamber in the Wakefield Tower. The king's throne stands behind the red rope on the left. Henry VI, the Lancastrian king, was murdered – probably by the Yorkist Edward IV – at the oratory where his portrait is displayed. On the anniversary of his death representatives of Eton College and King's College, Cambridge, which he founded, lay tributes of lilies and roses here.

Opposite The White Tower: a view through battlements of Tower Bridge (built 1893)

was to become one of the great honours of state, had a very practical origin. While kings themselves were not over fond of washing all over, the average squire simply stank and to have had a number of such newly made knights in close and continuous contact with the monarch after the ceremony of knighting was more than even they could countenance. The Ceremony of the Bath which took place after Richard's abdication followed a now long-established form, and one which would continue for centuries. Forty-six men were to be knighted. Forty-six tubs were prepared on the first floor of the White Tower in what were once the royal apartments adjoining St John's Chapel, and in the same chamber were forty-six beds. The postulant knights were immersed and thoroughly tubbed, at which stage the king entered the chamber in solemn procession, proceeding to each postulant as he knelt in his tub, hands piously clasped. On the back of each, the king made the sign of the Cross, dedicating the postulant to the service of Christ and of his king, and to the defence of the defenceless.

After the king withdrew the knights were dried, then rested in their beds before proceeding to the gruelling part of the ceremony, the Vigil. At curfew, signalled by the clanging of the great bell on what was already known as the Bell Tower, they arose, dressed themselves in coarse woollen habits and, in their turn, went in procession to St John's Chapel where they spent the night kneeling in prayer, each before his own dedicated armour, complete with everything except the sword. The following morning they joined the king in the palace where he formally presented them with their swords, that ultimate badge of Northern nobility and manhood. Fully accoutred now as knights of the realm, they then accompanied their king on his coronation procession to Westminster.

One man who did not take part in that procession was the late king, Richard II. Jean Froissart, the courtly French chronicler who had personally known and liked him ('He made me good cheer because in my youth I had been secretary to King Edward his grandfather') sadly recorded his mysterious end: 'It was not long after this that a true report was current in London of the death of Richard of Bordeaux. I could not learn the particulars of it, nor how it happened'. He believed that Richard had died in the Tower, but in that he was mistaken for Henry had discreetly moved

A highly fanciful version of Richard II's arrest. He was never actually imprisoned in the Tower although his body lay in state there.

Richard to Pontefract and it was there that he was probably murdered. But Henry gave him a good sending-off, bringing him back to the Tower where some 20,000 people saw him lying in state 'on a litter, his head on a black cushion, and his face uncovered' before being taken to Westminster Abbey for burial. He was just thirty-two years old.

Non-English royalty passed steadily through the Tower, usually as prisoners, their ultimate fate depending on the pressures in the outside world as well as the personality of their captors. Thus Griffith, Prince of Wales, might well have lived to a ripe, if boring, old age in the White Tower if he had not tried to escape by the same means that Flambard had done, by making a rope of sheets. 'But in sliding down the weight of his body, being a very big and fat man, brake the rope and he fell on his neck. Whose miserable carcarse being found in the morning by the Tower Wall, was a most pitiful sight to behold for his head and neck were driven into his breast, between the shoulders'.

John Baliol, king of Scotland, attempted nothing so foolish. Captured by Edward I – that famous Hammer of the Scots – he lived very comfortably in the White Tower on a literally princely allowance of seventeen shillings a day – paid by the king, though cannily deducted from Baliol's own estates. In due course, Edward pardoned him and actually granted him a pension. William Wallace was less generously treated, perhaps because so powerful a personality constituted too great a threat. Captured near Glasgow in 1305, he was 'tried' in Westminster Hall, and at Smithfield under the eyes of the Tower garrison he suffered the full barbaric punishment of being 'hung in a noose and afterwards let down living, his privates cut off and his bowels torn out and burnt'.

Under Edward III the flood of royal and noble prisoners accelerated, French as well as Scottish. Loot was, for the ordinary soldier, a primary reason for risking his skin in war but, further up the scale, ransom was as potent an attraction for his social superior. The higher the social level of a prisoner, the greater was his value – and thus the greater his chances of surviving a given battle. In 1346 David II, king of Scotland, captured at the battle of Nevilles Cross, was brought to London and underwent a weary eleven years' imprisonment until his devoted followers were able to raise the vast sum of one hundred thousand marks for his ransom, even though his wife was the sister of the English king.

David was in the last year of his imprisonment when the Tower received its most exalted – and thus most valuable – prisoner of all time: no less a person than John II, king of that great neighbouring country of France with whom the English lived in a permanent, painful, love-hate relationship. Captured by Edward's son, the Black Prince, at Poitiers in 1356 his arrival in London seemed more like the triumphant procession of a visiting monarch, than the entry of a prisoner. Mounted on a white horse, surrounded by members of his own court (who, in the aggregate, represented a very substantial sum in potential ransom) King John rode through a wildly enthusiastic crowd of onlookers. Reality came back at the Tower where a blacksmith, Andrew le Fevre, had made a specially designed grill for his room. For the London mob, in cheering the handsome man on a white horse, had seen him not only as the king of France but as the living, moving representative of three million florins, the incredible sum at which his ransom had been assessed. Somehow, the sum was raised even though France's currency was grotesquely devalued to allow it and the king was released in 1360 – but returned voluntarily three years later when his own son broke a parole. On this occasion he was housed, more as guest than as prisoner, in the Palace of the Savoy where he fell ill and died.

The last notable French prisoner was that Charles, duke of Orleans, who was captured at Agincourt in 1415, the battle which Shakespeare turned into a glorious triumph but was, in effect, the swan-song of the English monarchy's attempt to control France, the land of its origins. Charles was twenty-four when he was captured: he was forty-nine when his ransom, the then equal of some fifty thousand pounds, was paid and, looking back over his twenty-five years of imprisonment, he voiced the thought that occurs to most long-term prisoners: 'I have many a time wished that I had been slain at the battle where they took me'. The young duke, though one of the joint Commanders-in-Chief at the battle, was quite unsuited for a military life. Literature was his preferred interest, poetry his great love and during those endless days in the Tower of London he brought his art to a high pitch. The usually penny-pinching Henry VII had these poems bound into a magnificent illuminated copy to give as a present to his bride, Elizabeth of York, marking their marriage and the end of the Wars of the Roses. One of the splendid illuminations (see right) shows the duke of Orleans as a prisoner in the Tower, thus providing us with our first, clear picture of the Tower of London.

The illumination shows the Tower and its surrounds not as they appeared at the time of Charles's imprisonment, but as they would have appeared a little before 1486, the date of marriage of Henry and Elizabeth. In the background is London Bridge, crowded with houses and with the water roaring through the narrow arches which made 'shooting the bridge' (passing under it by boat) a hazardous occupation for centuries to come. Although the City in the background looks somewhat fanciful, the probability is that the unknown but highly skilful artist was depicting the towers and spires of the medieval town that existed before the Great Fire of the seventeenth century. By contrast, every detail of the Tower is recognizable today, allowing for the artist's adjustments of their relationship to tell his dramatic story. In the foreground is the stone wharf, built in 1389 to replace, at last, the old Roman wharf: at this period it is still, apparently, unpaved which would give some substance to the endless complaints of the Tower authorities about the stink emanating from the rubbish dumped in the surrounding area. Dominant in the foreground is the watergate, St Thomas's Tower, which Edward I built in the 1290s to replace the old watergate (not visible here for it stands immediately behind the new watergate). The artist seems to have given an almost deliberately anthropomorphic appearance to St Thomas's Tower, turning it into an ogre with glaring eyes, with the arch of the Traitors' Gate beneath an engulfing mouth.

Dominating the whole picture is the gleaming mass of the White Tower with a smaller tower of the same colour in front: the now vanished Wardrobe Tower (or, if this is the south side, the entrance to the keep) – evidently important enough at the time to be associated with the White Tower itself. The human figures in the painting tell a consecutive story. The duke is distinguished by

The duke of Orleans in the Tower

his collar of ermine. In the White Tower he is first shown writing his poems at a desk. He then appears looking out at a window, presumably observing the approach of those who have come, at last, to release him. Next he is in the courtyard, greeting a messenger who respectfully dips a knee while a servant brings up a horse already saddled and bridled. And finally his back view is shown, riding off to freedom after half his lifetime has been spent in captivity.

If we owe the first, clear, pictorial representation of the Tower to Henry VII we owe the first, relatively full, description of it to his son Henry VIII. But it is only relative for though, as a surveyor's report, it is far more accurate than the subjective accounts by chroniclers and others in the past, it is still tantalizingly patchy. And that is particularly unfortunate for Henry VIII was the last monarch to use the Tower as a royal palace. His reason for doing so is both obvious and sensible. England was poised on the brink of that great building boom which, created by increased wealth and a stabilized monarchy, would transform gloomy medieval manor houses and castles all over the country into the first of the 'stately homes' – the country houses of the English nobility. Henry was not going to be overshadowed by his own splendid chancellor, Cardinal Wolsey, who, in the 1520s, was busily engaged in creating his opulent palace of Hampton Court as well as expanding his London home of York Place in Westminster. In due course, Henry grabbed both, turning York Place into Whitehall Palace, strengthening yet again the pull of Westminster against the City, and, during the course of his reign, acquired or built eleven more palaces in and around London. These new, airy buildings with their towering windows and civilized sanitation, set among green fields and woods, were a world distant from the cramped, smelly, stone castle hemmed in by narrow streets crowded with people.

Nevertheless, it was still His Grace's Tower of London, the key to his capital city, with five centuries of tradition behind it, and a massive programme of work was put in hand to restore and refurbish the palace within the Tower, as well as some of the fortifications which were in considerable decay. The actual work was done under the supervision of Thomas Cromwell, Wolsey's successor. Meticulous bureaucrat that he was he demanded and received reports on the progress of work and, from them, one can obtain some idea of the layout of the now vanished palace.

Six of the chambers are specifically assigned to the king: his Great Watching Chamber (the guardroom for his personal bodyguard): his Great Chamber for ceremonial receptions: his Dining Chamber: a curious 'chamber where His Grace doth make him ready' – presumably a dressing room: a Closet which, furnished with an altar and praying stool, evidently served as his private chapel: and his Privy Chamber. The queen, too, had her own Great Chamber for ceremonies and a Dining Chamber. The 1597 plan of the Tower shows that she also had that great Tudor luxury, the Long Gallery, where exercise could be taken under cover on inclement days and this, in its turn, led to her private garden.

Two other major changes were made to the castle during Henry's reign. In 1512 the ancient church of St Peter ad Vincula was almost totally destroyed by fire and this was rebuilt in the contemporary manner with a splendid roof of Spanish chestnut and tall, handsome windows. Ironically, the little church received this elegant transformation at just about the time it was to become a species of necropolis for those beheaded on Tower Hill or within the Tower itself. The Tudor architectural characteristics are also evident in the range of buildings immediately to the right of the Bloody Tower. This is an L-shaped block, running from just inside the Bloody Tower arch (and therefore just outside the palace complex itself) to the corner near the Bell Tower and, from there, running north almost up to the Beauchamp Tower. Traditionally, this has always been known as the Queen's House, or the King's House, depending upon the sex of the monarch, but was, in fact, built as the residence of the Lieutenant of the Tower, whence its older name of the Lieutenant's Lodgings. Today it is the home of the Resident Governor and in all the vast expanse of the Tower of London, its exterior is the only one to present that residential appearance which was as much a characteristic of the Tower as its more obviously sombre, martial appearance.

The programme of work on the palace began in early 1532. By the spring of the following year, there was an increasing urgency about it for the king had decreed that all must be in readiness for the coronation of his new queen. That was to take place in May and, as tradition decreed, the new queen was to spend the previous night in the Tower before leaving in procession for Westminster Abbey.

On Thursday 28 May 1533 Queen Anne Boleyn was conducted, with unprecedented pomp, from the king's new palace of Greenwich just across the river to the splendid new royal apartments in the Tower. That night, eighteen nobles were made Knights of the Bath in her honour 'and were bathed and shreven accordyng to the old usage of England'. The next day, Whitsun Eve, Anne left for her coronation in a spectacular procession, travelling in an open litter drawn by two palfreys. She was dressed in white, her black hair hanging down to her waist as was the privilege of royalty, and on her head was a coif surmounted with a golden circlet encrusted with precious stones. Twelve noblemen, from the embassy of that French court where Anne had spent her youth, led the procession. After them came gentlemen, knights, esquires, two by two, all richly dressed. Next came the judges and the Knights of the Bath 'in violet gowns with hoods purfelled with miniver like doctors'. Yet more nobles and knights followed. Preceding the queen was her Chancellor: two knights held a canopy of cloth-of-gold over her head: her huge personal staff of servants and officers brought up the rear of the procession. Musicians enlivened the way and along the route fountains flowed with red and white wines. The Londoners, however, normally only too pleased to welcome any kind of display, were curiously silent, which displeased her. But her doting husband was waiting at the Abbey to enfold her in his arms and make her, as by law and custom, his queen.

Three years later Queen Anne Boleyn was to return to the Tower of London under rather different conditions.

Anne's stay at the Tower on the night preceding her coronation, and the subsequent procession from Tower to Abbey, was the last occasion on which that tradition was observed until Charles II briefly revived it. After her departure, the Tower became 'rather an armorie and house of munition, and thereunto a place for the safe-keeping of offenders, than a palace roiall for a king or queen to soiourein in', in Holinshed's sombre words. And none was more responsible for turning it into 'a place for the safe-keeping of offenders' than the, at that time, doting husband of Anne Boleyn.

SECTION II
THE PRISON

Now, for King Henry VIII, if all the pictures and patterns of a merciless prince were lost in the world, they might all again be painted out of the story of this king. For, how many servants did he advance in haste and, with the change of his fancy, ruin again? To how many others, of more desert, gave he abundant flowers from whence to gather honey, and in the end of harvest burned them in the hive? How many wives did he cut off, and cast off, as his fancy and affection changed? How many princes of the blood (whereof some of them for age could scarcely crawl towards the block), with a world of others of all degree did he execute?

Sir Walter Raleigh
Preface to *The History of the World*

CHAPTER IV
THE GRAND GUIGNOL OF KING HENRY VIII

It is one of history's more profound ironies and puzzles that the murderous pedant, Henry VIII, should emerge with the soubriquet of 'Bluff King Hal' as though his worst characteristics were an excess of energy and an indifference to table manners. It is, perhaps, because the memory of the golden youth overlays that of the gross and vicious man. We remember Holbein's portrait of the splendidly dressed prince, pulsing with vitality and with a kind of amiable aggressiveness, and not Cornelius Matys's portrait, painted three years before Henry's death at the early age of fifty-six, with its sly, sinister, sideways glance, its gross, flabby cheeks and mean, prissy little mouth. (One wonders, indeed, how Matys got away with it.) Posterity does well to take a very close look at received historical judgements, standing them on their heads if need be to see how they look in that perspective, for received historical judgements are only too often based on the propaganda of victors, or the reaction of hindsight. Posterity might well wonder whether Richard III was quite the misshapen monster of total evil as appeared in Shakespearean/Tudor propaganda or, conversely, whether the saintly Thomas More, for all his hair shirt and family love, was quite the Christlike figure of Catholic reaction. But in the matter of King Henry VIII, posterity has been handed a sketch which, though over coloured, is accurate enough in its outline.

Visitors to the site of the scaffold on Tower Green frequently express surprise – and, it would seem, a touch of disappointment – that only seven people were beheaded there, but a simple analysis of the identity of the victims adds a peculiar dimension of horror. Only two of the seven were men – Lord Hastings and the Earl of Essex – both of whom were involved in conspiracy, or active

The proprietor of the Grand Guignol: King Henry VIII

rebellion, against a monarch. Of the five women, Lady Jane Grey was the pawn of an unscrupulous family whose ambitions threatened civil war. The remaining four women were victims of Henry VIII, three of whom were involved in his marital affairs and the fourth, an old woman in her sixties, murdered because she belonged to the dynasty which Henry's father had usurped.

The official guidebook to the Tower of London is at some pains to emphasize that the Tower's period as a prison was, on the whole, an aberrant lasting less than two centuries in the nine centuries of the castle's existence. 'An innocent visitor to the place today', says the guidebook, 'might be led to suppose by guides and guidebooks that it was built almost entirely by Tudor monarchs, exclusively for the incarceration, torture and execution of their innumerable prisoners. In truth this is a grossly misleading exaggeration of what is, in the main, a late and temporary phase in the history of the Tower'.

The guidebook's indignation is justified, for the Tower's Grand Guignol period lasted less than a quarter of its history to date and, even during that period, it discharged a vital and honourable function as an ordinary fortress. But neither is posterity unjustified in regarding the Tudor period as one of peculiar horror – a period initiated by Bluff King Hal. His four victims slaughtered within the secrecy of the Tower walls are far outnumbered by the twenty-three others who went to their deaths by axe on Tower Hill, or the unknown numbers of lesser folk who died by the noose at Tyburn, during his reign.

But apart from the results of the king's desire for vengeance, or his Byzantine twists and turns to establish legality where legality could not possibly exist (as, for instance, his argument that his marriage to Anne Boleyn was null and void because he had beforehand committed adultery with her sister) Henry VIII contributed a new and dizzying twist to the processes that filled the dungeons of the Tower. That twist was the religious. Hitherto, most prisoners landed in the Tower simply because they had backed the losing side in the endless struggle for power. Now, a subtle interpretation of theology – an interpretation which could change year by year or even month by month – could have the same result. In the beginning Henry had merely, in effect, moved the goalposts and murdered those who either argued that the goalposts should not be moved on a unilateral decision, or who continued to play the game as though the posts were in their original place. Thomas More, for instance, was perfectly prepared to recognize the Act of Succession, whereby the children of Henry's new marriage could alone inherit the crown for this, he said, was a decree made by parliament. He could not, however, recognize the Oath of Supremacy, whereby Henry became Head of the Church for, said he, 'I am unable to change my conscience and conform to the Council of one realm against the General Council of Christendom'. It was a perfectly logical argument, and one indeed which Henry had tacitly used when writing his ponderous refutation of Martin Luther which, ironically, gained him the title of 'Defender of the Faith' from a grateful pope. But that was in the past. Henry, who would have fitted happily into George Orwell's *1984*, now required More to say that truth had changed in the interim. More refused to do so, and Henry killed him for it.

That was a straightforward act of tyranny, but as the century advanced and the struggle polarized and hardened, it became increasingly difficult for the adherents of the Italian priest in Rome not to be the automatic enemy of the English monarch in London. Thus, in 1588, the Catholic earl of Arundel openly rejoiced at the impending destruction of his queen and the subjection of his country: 'He was still confined in the Tower when the Spanish Armada entered the Channel and could not forebeare expressing his joy at the news. He had likewise caused a Mass of the Holy Ghost to be said for its success'. Fourteen years later occurred the Gunpowder Plot, today celebrated as a 'colourful heritage' but, in fact, an appallingly bloodthirsty plan which would not only have murdered the supposedly guilty James I and his cronies, but also several score innocents – including a number of Catholics. When the tables were turned the reverse, of course, applied – and the turned tables did not even have to bring a Catholic monarch to the throne, as with Henry's daughter Mary. The Puritan fanatics of the seventeenth century were as eager to see minor deviations from their ferocious creeds punished by incarceration in the Tower as they were to rejoice in the destruction of the more obviously ungodly. Henry VIII had opened a Pandora's Box which did not even have Hope at the bottom: exhaustion alone eventually brought peace.

Apart from the Conqueror himself, no other occupant of the English throne so altered the course of English history as this Welshman. When, at the age of eighteen, he succeeded his parsimonious, sly father England might well feel that this handsome, blond youth with the expansive manner was the very epitome of the new spirit, that very Renaissance which was sweeping Europe with its warmth and its light: 'Heaven and earth rejoices: everything is full of milk and honey and nectar. Avarice has fled the country. Our king is not after gold, or gems, or precious metals but virtue, glory, immortality'. Boisterous, ebullient but cultured, passionately fond of music and a skilled musician: well educated – though not, perhaps, as widely and deeply as he thought, particularly in the field of theology – combining all this with personal courage and a seemingly inexhaustible energy that allowed him to ride nonstop for hours at a time, he seemed the first of the new breed of universal man.

But there was already visible, to those that had the eyes to see, something of the instability that would turn his closing years into a nightmare for those around him. He had never been trained in the arts of government, for that had been reserved for his elder brother Arthur: he had never made decisions, had been kept cloistered from the world – so much so that a Venetian remarked that he might have been a nun in a nunnery. This green youth emerged to a situation of absolute power, tempered at first by a council of elders. But, as the years went by, so the monstrous ego developed until Henry fell at last to the lure dangled before all of his class and period: caesaro-papism, to be both emperor and pope, both priest and king.

When Sir Thomas More's son-in-law congratulated him for his closeness with the king – Henry had been seen with his arm around More's neck – More replied soberly, 'I think he doth as singularly favour me as any subject within this realm. Howbeit, I have no great cause to be proud thereof. If my head could win his Majesty a castle in France – it should not fail to go'. More had seen the killer behind the mask of Bluff King Hal clearly enough: his predecessor as Chancellor, Cardinal Wolsey, had escaped the block only through a timely natural death, for Wolsey had committed the penultimate sin, he had failed. Inescapably, More

Sir Thomas More: 'If my head could win his Majesty a castle in France – it should not fail to go'

was driven into a position where he had to commit the ultimate sin, defying the monarch.

In the matter of Henry's divorce, More had been, if anything, a supporter: if the daughter of the Borgia pope could obtain a divorce, as she had just a generation earlier, there was no real reason why the king of England should be denied. 'There are some who say that the King is pursuing a divorce out of love for some lady, and not out of scruple of conscience – but this is not true,' More told parliament. 'The King hath not attempted this matter of will or pleasure, but only from the discharge of conscience and surety of the succession of his realm.' There was, in fact, a perfectly legitimate heiress, Mary, daughter of the unfortunate Katherine of Aragon, but this was not good enough for the king. As far as Henry's divorce and subsequent marriages are concerned, it is all but impossible to disentangle his motives, to distinguish the sexual from the political, the political from the religious. The delectable, twenty-six-year-old Anne Boleyn was undoubtedly a more attractive proposition than the ageing, dowdy Queen Katherine, six years older than her husband. But there was also the very real hope that the younger woman might produce that heir so vital to maintain the stability of a country in the throes of transition. More could go along with that, telling Thomas Cromwell, Henry's bull-necked secretary, that he was among 'His Grace's faithful subjects, his Highness being in possession of his marriage and this noble woman [Anne Boleyn] really anointed queen, neither murmur at it nor dispute upon it'. Then Henry moved the goalposts, requiring from More – above all his subjects – the Oath of Supremacy recognizing the king as the head of the church.

On 17 April 1534 More was led into the Tower as a prisoner. On 6 July 1535 he was led out to his death.

It is rare that posterity has a clear and utterly incontrovertible illustration of the effect of even fourteen months' imprisonment than in the portraits of Thomas More before, and approaching the end of, his imprisonment. For his appearance before, we have Hans Holbein's unforgettable portrait of him: the long, pointed, inquisitive nose, the mobile, humorous mouth, the laughter crinkles around the eyes, all reflect his friend Erasmus's kindly description of his face as being 'more suggestive of gaiety than dignity or serious gravity', despite his vast learning and heavy responsibilities. Contrast that portrait with the one made, by an anonymous artist, some little time before the end. Under the black cap his face is pale and haggard, the eyes sunken, their expression sombre: the crisp, facial stubble has become a long, straggling beard. The only recognizable detail is the mouth, though its expression now is wry, resigned.

More's cell was on the ground floor of the Bell Tower, so called because it held the garrison's alarm bell. Built about the year 1200 it marked the then furthest expansion of the castle to the west and was correspondingly massive. In More's time, as today, it had no external access, the only way in, and out, being through the Lieutenant's Lodgings which it adjoined – a good place to keep a very important prisoner. The Bell Tower had one other advantage

Sir Thomas More's cell in the basement of the Bell Tower – an unheated stone box. Compare this with Raleigh's accommodation (page 70).

from the gaoler's point of view: there was no communication between the lower and upper floors – an important point, for the upper floor held another distinguished prisoner of conscience, Bishop Fisher of Rochester. More owed his imprisonment to the fact that he kept silence, that he would not swear that Oath of Supremacy: Fisher owed his to the fact that he had talked too much. Not only had he opposed the king, but he had openly supported Elizabeth Barton, the 'Holy Maid of Kent'. The Holy Maid was one of those religious fanatics who were to become wearisomely common over the following two centuries of religious strife. Her epileptic fits gave dramatic emphasis to her outbursts against the king and his 'Bullen whore' and a cult rapidly built up around the Holy Maid. She, and her immediate associates, were adequately dealt with at Tyburn. Bishop Fisher ended up in the Bell Tower above Thomas More for, like More, punishment alone was not sufficient: what was required was actual submission and wholehearted recantation. In other words to agree, as Winston Smith was obliged to agree in *1984*, that two and two really did make five.

The confinement of More and Fisher was not, in the beginning, particularly rigorous. More, certainly, was not only allowed visits from his family but was actually allowed to stroll in the Lieutenant's garden with them. His son-in-law wrote a vivid account of a conversation More had with his wife, Dame Alice. She, poor lady, was puzzled by what all the fuss was about. ' "What, in God's name you mean to tarry here?" With a cheerful countenance he said to her – "Mrs Alice, tell me one thing". "What is that?", quoth she. "Is not this house as near heaven as my own?" Whereto after her accustomed homely fashion she answered – "Tille valle, tille valle. Good God man, will your old tricks never be left".'

There were official visitors, too, among them Thomas Cromwell, Henry's secretary. Cromwell has had a bad press as the king's bully boy, the man who engineered the destruction of the monasteries, a reputation made worse by the devastatingly honest portrait by Holbein which emphasized his brutal strength. Yet he served his country well according to his lights, desperately trying to hold together a society seemingly bent on destroying itself through centrifugal force. Apart from the professional need to win submission from the ex-Chancellor and so gain his master's gratitude

Thomas Cromwell, earl of Essex: 'I am no traitor'

– or what passed for Henry's gratitude – he seems to have been genuinely fond of More, genuinely wished to bring him into what was now the mainstream of politics. More declined with his misleadingly lighthearted manner and the screws began to be tightened upon both More and Fisher and even as the two portraits of More provide illustrated testimony of the rigours of imprisonment, so does Fisher's pathetic letter to Cromwell provide documentary evidence. More was fifty-seven, and in good health, but poor Fisher was an old man, approaching his eighties and, apparently, without the financial resources that enabled More's family to keep him well supplied with food and drink and warm clothes:

> I beseech you to be a good master unto my necessite [he wrote pleadingly to Cromwell]. I have neither shirt, nor suit, nor yett other clothes that ar necessary for me to weare, but that they be ragged and rent so shamefully. Notwithstanding, I might easily suffer that, if thei wold keep my body warm. But my diet also, God knoweth how slender it is at many times. And now, in myn age, my stomach may not away but with a few kynd of meats which, if I lack, I decaye forthwith and fall into coughs and diseases of my bodye. And, as our Lord knoweth, I have nothying left unto me for to provyde any better, but as my brother of his own purse layeth out.

There is no record as to whether Master Cromwell was stirred by this piteous plea. It seems unlikely and, in any case, their spiritual master, the foxy Pope Paul III, settled the affairs of both men by creating Fisher a cardinal. Until then, it seems as though Henry was content to let both men simply rot in gaol, but so direct a challenge to the English Crown sent him into a paroxysm of rage, bellowing that Fisher would have no head upon which to put the red hat. No longer were these two men theological deviants: they were traitors and he wanted them executed as such. There was little difficulty in building up a case against Fisher and after a trial that was little more than a formality he was beheaded on Tower Hill. As a traitor, his head was placed on a spike on London Bridge while the headless corpse was buried in the nearby church of All Hallows. Evidently it became a focus of pilgrimage, for shortly afterwards it was disinterred and tumbled into a nameless grave in that macabre dumping ground for state victims, the chapel of St Peter ad Vincula in the Tower itself. So ended the most illustrious of the first wave of religious victims.

It proved far more difficult to entrap More for he was no talkative old priest, but a canny lawyer who knew the value of silence. Cromwell's interrogations took place in the Great Council Chamber of the White Tower where he could, simultaneously, display himself in the full panoply of Vicar-General – in effect, deputy head of the church in England – while maintaining a careful control of events. At one stage More was even invited to sit alongside his interrogators as though on equal terms – for after all, were they not old fellow-Councillors of his? He saw the trap and courteously avoided it. They got him in the end through the device of the *agent provocateur*. William Rich, a man who owed his advancement to More, entered More's cell while he was writing and, during the course of what appeared to be simply an academic debate on the nature of lawful authority, managed to extract a statement from More which appeared to suggest that he denied the king's authority. Two witnesses who were packing up More's books at the time refused to sign Rich's deposition, declaring it a perjury, but it was good enough to pass as evidence in a Tudor court.

The interrogations had taken place in the secrecy of the Tower, but the trial itself was to be held, in a blaze of publicity, in that great Westminster Hall where More himself had so often presided as Chancellor. Those who saw him as he stumbled along on his three-mile via Dolorosa from the City of London to the City of Westminster were shocked and startled by his emaciated appearance: in the space of some fourteen months a healthy, vigorous man in his prime had been transformed into a broken old man who had occasionally to be supported by the halberdiers who hemmed him round. The return journey was made by river, but between leaving Westminster Hall (where one of his judges had been Anne Boleyn's father) and boarding the boat, the eyes of the crowd that witnessed his passage were turned to one object – the gleaming, crescent-shaped ceremonial axe held high above the sombre procession. The blade was turned towards the victim.

At Tower Pier, More's son and daughter fought their way through the halberdiers and knelt at their father's feet. He was returned to the Bell Tower and, five days later, on 6 July 1535 was led out to his death. He had already been told that the king 'in his gracious mercy' had decided that he should not suffer the full hideous ritual of hanging, disembowelling and quartering at Tyburn but would be executed as a gentleman at Tower Hill. 'God forbid the King shall use any more such mercy on any of my friends', he replied, or was later reported as replying, for Thomas More's departure from life was to be the subject of colourful embroidery as he emerged to the status of saint and of symbol. A woman was supposed to have offered him a glass of wine, which he refused for Christ had had vinegar and gall. Another, with a certain lack alike of tact and of commonsense, demanded that he return some papers she had sent him as Lord Chancellor. The scaffold was rickety and he turned to the Lieutenant accompanying him, 'I pray you see me safely up and for my coming down let me shift for myself'. Bluffly, he cheered up the executioner, who begged his forgiveness: 'I forgive thee – but prithee let me put my beard aside, for that hath never committed treason'. Of all the apocryphal remarks, that was the most unlikely, for at no stage had he ever admitted to treason. But even when all these are discounted, it is evident that, despite Martin Luther's sour remark – 'He was a very notable tyrant who shed the blood of many innocent Christians that confessed the Gospel' – Sir Thomas More left life as he had lived it, with gaiety and courage and style, and with the tears of those who knew him. The headless body went to join the ever-growing number in the castle's chapel; the head was spiked on London Bridge until More's remarkable daughter Margaret managed to retrieve it and give it a decent burial in the little church of St Dunstan in Canterbury.

A year later, the 'Bullen whore', cause of the tide of blood that was beginning to lap around the Tower, lay under sentence of death within it.

Of all the marital tangles of Henry VIII, the reasons for his repudiation of the wife for whom he had altered the course of English history, are obscure. Did he really believe that she had committed incest with her brother? Did he really believe that she had committed adultery 'with an hundred men' and had been stupid enough to name a successor to him? On the night of her arrest, did he really clutch his illegitimate son to him, sobbing that 'that damned strumpet' had planned to poison both the boy and his halfsister Mary? If he did not believe these things, and it is scarcely conceivable that he did, then Anne Boleyn was, quite simply, murdered.

There was some brutal justification for the later execution of Katherine Howard: she had undoubtedly been guilty of adultery and might therefore very likely have introduced a bastard into the dynasty with the likelihood of future chaos and bloodshed. But Anne Boleyn steadfastly protested her innocence of this particular charge, even at the awesome moment when she took communion before her death.

Looking into the maelstrom of Tudor politics – in particular those involving Bluff King Hall – posterity is in the position of someone looking down into an aquarium filled with murky, but not quite opaque water, in which ferocious creatures battle for dominance and for survival. Occasionally one will come to the surface, giving a brief glimpse of jaws and teeth and claws; inspecting the wounds on the corpses of the slain one can deduce the course of the battle, the turbulence on the surface of the water some indication of its ferocity. But it is impossible to follow any one engagement, assigning simple clear-cut motives. In that murderous aquarium, Anne Boleyn was both victim and predator, victim to the larger monsters, predator among the smaller creatures. She had revelled in her role of queen, believing that its high-sounding title wrapped her around in security. And so it did, save in one vital direction – the threat from her husband.

Anne Boleyn: 'I have heard say the executioner is very good and I have a little neck'

Anne Boleyn provides a classic example of the fact that sexual attraction is not necessarily related to physical beauty. The Venetian ambassador, penning one of those coldly clinical reports on human beings which made his government one of the best informed in history, said of her, 'Mistress Anne is not the handsomest woman in the world. She is of middle height, dark-skinned, long-necked, wide mouth, bosom not much raised'. She had, he thought, most beautiful eyes. Anne's most famous portrait, by an unknown artist, bears out much of the Italian's comments: the most notable features, indeed, are that long, slender neck, and the black eyes. But the portrait conveys something about Anne which is quite lacking in the portraits of Henry's other wives, even the vivacious eighteen-year-old Katherine Howard: there is a kind of sparkle about her expression, as if she is just holding herself in for the duration of the sitting and will be off on some exciting new experience as soon as the painter has finished.

And that, in fact, was one of the characteristics which brought her to the block. Effervescent, hungry for flattery, delighting in male company, convinced that she entirely captivated her husband and so was free to experiment, she conducted herself with a lack of discretion which would have aroused the mistrust of a less morose man than her husband. And Henry, despite that reputation as satyr which he bequeathed to history as a result of his six marriages, was almost certainly sexually inadequate. Initially, Anne undoubtedly enthralled him, able to hold him off at arm's length until she brought him to the pitch whereby he would turn off his current wife and turn English history upon its head. And the first few months of marriage would have been a continuation of the enthralment, for she was still in her early twenties and, after having spent all of her young womanhood first in the court of France, and then that of England, undoubtedly knew the skills that would keep alive the interests of a man many years her senior whose powers were already fading through disease and self-indulgence.

But the skills were not, quite, enough to counterbalance the sharp tongue and the shrewish temper. The larger predators in the aquarium smelt blood as the king's attention began to wander. And she had no allies, neither in the court, nor in the country. The Spanish ambassador had reported, to his king, a curious aspect about her otherwise triumphant coronation procession. On her arrival at Westminster, the besotted king had taken her in his arms, asking her how she liked the city. 'Sir, I liked the city well enough,' the ambassador reported her as saying, 'but I saw a great many caps on heads and heard but few tongues.' 'It is a thing to note', the ambassador pointed out 'that the common people always disliked her.'

The 'common people's' dislike was based on a general objection to the manner in which 'the old queen' – Katherine of Aragon – had been thrust aside for this upstart. The dislike of the court, of those who came into actual, daily contact with the new queen, was more personal, more venomous and, in the long run, far more dangerous. For Anne Boleyn had fallen into the trap that awaits the parvenue – the loss of perspective. Secure, as she thought, in the king's adoration, she indulged in the pleasures of the small minded, the pleasures that appeal to the serving maid who suddenly finds herself literally queening it in the mistress's chamber. Her attitude towards her wretched sixteen-year-old stepdaughter, Mary, daughter of the humiliated and repudiated Katherine of Aragon, was shameful, for the unfortunate girl was obliged to act as maid to her baby halfsister, Elizabeth. But all those around Anne who were in a subservient position found themselves smarting under the lash of her tongue. And as Henry's passion cooled, as pregnancy succeeded pregnancy and the only produce was yet another girl child, as his thoughts and attentions turned elsewhere, to another possible vessel to contain a future king of England so the predators rapidly began to gather around Anne, the queen, who would remain the queen just so long as she could detain the attention of her husband and not a moment longer. Her enemies assembled, not simply because they disliked her or disapproved of her, but because he who could place a woman in the king's marital bed had placed a most valuable pawn upon the political board.

On May Day 1536, that happiest day of all the year when all the world went out to celebrate the greening of spring, the king and queen were at a tournament at the royal palace of Greenwich on the Thames. A handful of watchers, who kept a very close observation on the king, noted with satisfaction a courtier approach him and hand him a letter. The king read it, leaped up with a black face, ordered the jousting to halt and stormed off, leaving a puzzled and very apprehensive Queen Anne in the seat of honour on the royal balcony. She never saw her husband again. On the following day, at Greenwich, she was arrested, charged with adultery, taken to a boat and rowed the half mile or so upstream to the Tower of London, landing at the watergate which would soon earn the name of Traitors' Gate. On arrival there, she was in a state of hysteria.

Sir William Kingston, Constable of the Tower of London, was faced with a task of unusual delicacy. John Bayley, the somewhat puritanical if erudite nineteenth-century historian of the Tower, described him roundly as 'a base and obsequious minion: a man possessing neither heart nor principle'. But here John Bayley's partisanship betrays him, for all contemporaries of Kingston agree that he conducted his duty, during his sixteen-year tenure of the post of Constable, with chivalry and compassion for the unhappy wretches over whose departure from the world he was obliged to preside. He had, in fact, excellent reason for disliking Anne Boleyn for he had been a close personal friend of Sir Thomas More and More's death could, with justice, be attributed to her. But he greeted the terrified young woman with the same grave courtesy with which he treated all alike. His problem lay in deciding just what treatment should be accorded a queen of England who was also a prisoner, a situation quite without precedent. The evil reputation the Tower had already acquired is demonstrated by Anne's first quavering question, 'Mr Kingston, shall I go into a dungeon?' 'No, madam', Kingston replied, 'You shall go into your lodgings that you lay in at your coronation'.

Kingston's answer creates an historical puzzle. The 'lodgings' in which Anne stayed at the time of her coronation were undoubtedly in the now vanished palace. But a strong tradition of the Tower insists that she was imprisoned in the Lieutenant's Lodgings. The official guide even states (with a somewhat curious lack of uncertainty) that 'Of all the Tower ghosts, Anne's has been most often reported beneath the window of the room [in the Lodgings] where she spent her last days'. The contradiction can be resolved by assuming that Kingston moved her from the palace to the Lodgings where a close watch could be kept on her, for he had received most explicit instructions from Cromwell that Anne was not only to be placed under permanent surveillance, but every word she uttered must be written down to strengthen the decidedly weak case against her. She had a very large retinue, as befitted a still reigning queen of England – three waiting women, a page and two men. Her aunt, Lady Boleyn, and a Mrs Cosyn actually slept in her room and Kingston's wife, Lady Kingston, had a small room immediately next door. All the women in close contact with her were ordered to report everything of significance to Kingston who embodied these reports in a series of letters to Cromwell. We thus have a most unusually clear and comprehensive picture of how a prisoner reacted to the awful fate hanging over her.

Anne's initial reaction, on the steps of Traitors' Gate, was an almost mindless terror: 'She kneeled down, weeping apace, and in the same sorrow fell into a great laughing, which she hath done several times since'. From that she passed to self-delusion, convinced that she would eventually walk free – 'The King doth this to prove me' – or, at worst, be sent to a nunnery. But gradually she began to accept the reality of her situation and even to make that black joke about having 'a very little neck'. And all the time, she asserted her innocence: 'I am the king's true wedded wife.'

Meanwhile, the inexorable machinery began to turn over. Five men had been arrested with her: her brother Lord Rochford – charged with incest: Mark Smeaton, a lively and very popular young musician: Sir Francis Weston, whose father had been among the 'sad [ie sober] knights' who had acted as guides and tutors to Henry in his adolescence: a certain William Brereton: and Sir Henry Norris. All were accused of criminal misconduct with the queen. All, except Smeaton, denied the charge. Smeaton not only confessed to a criminal intimacy, but claimed that both Norris and Brereton had slept with the queen. Rumour had it that, on Cromwell's instructions, the 'confession' was extracted from him under torture and that seems the more likely explanation for there is no evidence that the three men, though doubtless guilty of a careless and, in the event, suicidal indiscretion, ever went beyond the bounds of the elaborate display tolerated by the unwritten rules of the traditional Courts of Love. Norris, Smeaton and Brereton were tried at Westminster Hall, found guilty and condemned to death, the two aristocrats by beheading on Tower Hill, the commoner Smeaton by the prolonged agony of strangulation at Tyburn. Curiously, a stay of execution was granted to them pending the result of Anne's trial. If, by some unlikely chance, she had been found not guilty then, logically, their sentence would have had to have been quashed – which would have placed Cromwell in a decidedly embarrassing position. Evidently, however, he was so confident of the result of a rigged trial that he felt free to give the appearance, at least, of justice, to the three men.

The trial of Anne and her brother took place, separately, in the Great Hall of the palace within the Tower, Anne's trial taking place first. Many of the twenty-six peers who were now her judges – including her uncle, the duke of Norfolk, who presided – were also her prosecutors for they had formed the Council which had formulated the charges against her. The public were admitted, including the Lord Mayor of London who was later to court death by courageously expressing his doubt as to her guilt. Spectacularly dressed in black and scarlet – a black velvet robe over a vivid scarlet kirtle, her waist-length black hair caught up under a pearl-trimmed head-dress, Anne swept into the Hall escorted by the Lieutenant. Anne Boleyn had many faults, but she lacked neither courage nor a sense of style, conducting herself with dignity as the travesty of a trial went on. History has been left a one-sided version of the trial, for the records of her own defence conveniently disappeared, the statements of her accusers alone being transmitted to posterity. It was left to her uncle, displaying that marvellous talent of his for survival, to pronounce sentence: 'Because thou hast offended our Sovereign the King's Grace in committing treason against his person, the law of the realm is this: that thou shalt be burnt here within the Tower of London, on this Green, else to have thy head smitten off as the king's pleasure shall be further known of the same'. Given the character of Bluff King Hal, the purely legal phrase 'the king's pleasure' took on a peculiarly sinister interpretation. In the event 'the king's pleasure' was for the quicker penalty.

Lord Rochford, Anne's brother, followed her into the Hall. Quite a number of the peers who now considered his case had previously 'wagered ten to one that he would be acquitted, especially as no witnesses were produced against him'. Obediently, and cannily, they now forgot their reservation and the young man was condemned with the rest.

William Kingston takes up the story again in his letters to Cromwell, seeking instructions, anxious to cover himself but also to act fairly towards his charges. The king was evidently in personal contact with Kingston, wanting the matter finished as swiftly as possible, for preparations for his next wedding were already far advanced. The queen, Kingston told Cromwell, 'said this day at dinner she should go to Hanover and is in hope of life'. Kingston disabused her of the idea as gently but as firmly as possible for although Archbishop Cranmer had obediently annulled her marriage (incidentally making her daughter, the future legendary Queen Elizabeth, a bastard) her continued existence would be an embarrassment to a newly married king. Thereafter she seems to have become resigned to a remarkable degree – 'This lady has much joy and pleasure in death' – making Kingston's task easier.

Kingston had many problems, among them 'the preparation of scaffolds and other necessaries'. This was to be the first, formal execution within the Tower. The beheading of Lord Hastings a quarter of a century before had been as unceremonious as cutting off the head of a chicken, a convenient length of timber doing duty for the block. A scaffold was to be built for Anne so that all could see that justice – such as it was – had been done. The king, through Cromwell, had made it clear that only a selected few should be present. Kingston replied that he had now expelled all strangers from the Tower – there had, in any case, only been about thirty. It would be best, he said, if the actual hour of the execution were kept uncertain. Another problem for the worried Constable was the execution itself. Anne had asked for the privilege of being beheaded by sword and the king had graciously consented but 'We have here no man for to do execution', for it took a skilled man to use the heavy execution sword – one of the reasons Anne had asked for the privilege instead of risking some clumsy butcher with an axe. It was decided to send to France for a swordsman. This, in turn, caused a delay and Kingston went to inform his prisoner. His letter to Cromwell describing his last interview with the queen of England does honour both to him and to his prisoner.

Anne had earlier requested his company at the time she took communion in order that she might declare her innocence at that solemn moment. She then went on:

> "Mr Kyngston, I hear say I shall not die before noon, and I am very sorry therefore: for I had thought to be dead now and past my pain" I told her it would be no pain, it was so subtle. Then she said "I have heard say the executioner is very good and I have a little neck" and putting her hand about it laughed heartily. I have seen many men and also women executed and that they have been in great sorrow and, to my knowledge, this lady has much joy and pleasure in death . . .

She was led out a little before noon, wearing a robe of grey damask with a low, loose collar which would not impede the swordsman, and walked the hundred yards or so from the Lieutenant's Lodgings to the scaffold with a firm, graceful step. The elaborate preparations for secrecy proved unnecessary for, to most people's surprise, her valedictory speech was short – 'I am not here to preach to you, but to die' – and conventional. Kneeling upright, for execution by the sword needed no block, her eyes were blindfolded and, with one efficient stroke, the swordsman removed her head. There was one oversight in Constable William Kingston's otherwise meticulous planning: no one had thought to provide a coffin. Hurriedly an arrow chest was brought from the armoury, the body was placed in it, one of the women who attended the queen picked up the head in a handkerchief and laid it beside the body. The chest and its contents were then lowered into a shallow grave in the chapel. The date was 19 May 1536. Ten days later, the king entered on his third marriage.

On 10 June 1540, exactly four years and three weeks since Anne Boleyn stepped on to the scaffold, the man who sent her there, Thomas Cromwell, was about to join his fellow Councillors for their midday meal. In what was evidently a carefully rehearsed series of events, the duke of Norfolk contemptuously shouldered him aside: 'It is not meet that traitors should sit among loyal gentlemen'. Astonished, beside himself with rage, the man who could now call himself earl of Essex, Lord Great Chamberlain, the confidant and right hand of King Henry VIII, snarled back, 'I am no traitor'. Even as he was speaking the door burst open and guards rushed in, seized him and bundled him down to a boat waiting by the Westminster watergate. Half an hour later he, too, had passed under the portcullis of the Traitors' Gate and was in the Tower of London. The most savage predator in the acquarium had, unaccountably, become a victim. But his fall was unaccountable only to outsiders. Insiders, like the duke of Norfolk who had bided his time before dealing with his enemy, knew that Cromwell had committed a crime only a degree or so less than the crime of defiance: he had failed the king.

Cromwell had come up the hard way, one of the new breed of self-made men who would make Tudor England great as a byproduct of their own drive to fortune. The son of a brewer, he served as a mercenary on the Continent before appearing in the retinue of Cardinal Wolsey. At some stage he picked up legal training and his advance under Wolsey's shadow was meteoric. After Wolsey's fall he attracted the attention of his king, for Thomas Cromwell – immensely able, utterly ruthless and totally devoted – was precisely the agent that Henry needed. Did His Grace require to replenish his coffers with the wealth of monasteries? Mr Secretary Cromwell was swift to devise the means. Did His Grace require the arraignment of a bishop, the discomfiture of a Chancellor or to be rid of an unwanted wife? Cromwell was at hand to bring about the desired end.

But Cromwell was also fighting his own corner. The internecine struggles, which were a feature of all medieval courts as their members strove to control their monarch, received an additional edge, an additional complication at Henry's court with the religious struggle. England had repudiated the pope – but it was by no means a Protestant country. The monolithic mould of the papacy had been broken, but the fragments took an individual life, as in some monstrous fable. On the extreme right were those like More and Fisher – fools or martyrs according to viewpoint – who refused to recognize change. Backed up by the outraged authority of the king, it had been easy enough to dispose of them. At the extreme left were those who repudiated all earthly powers, monarchs and priests alike: they too were easy to dispose of for they had not centre or head. It was in the middle ground that Cromwell fought his most ferocious battle. Right of centre were those, such as the duke of Norfolk, Catholics still but only too glad to hide their more extreme beliefs until a more sympathetic monarch occupied the throne. Norfolk had lost one pawn with his foolish niece Anne Boleyn and Cromwell's star had risen as the opposition's had fallen. But they bided their time, for opportunity would present itself. Opportunity came with the affair of Anne of Cleves. This, which was to be Cromwell's masterstroke, with the Crown of England united to a Protestant Continental house, proved his nemesis.

Holbein's portrait of Anne of Cleves, the spark which caused the explosion, is one of the many puzzles of the Tudor court. Holbein has been described by the art historians Peter and Lindsay Murray, as 'probably the most accomplished and penetrating realist portrait painter the North has produced'. He had been the official court painter for nearly seven years, producing that memorable series of portraits which has fixed Henry's court in the mind of posterity. He was specifically commissioned to produce a portrait of Anne of Cleves to allow Henry, who had never met the lady, to make up his mind about her. On seeing the portrait, Henry was bowled over with delight and eagerly assented to the marriage. Yet, when he met Anne in the flesh, he recoiled in disgust. Had Holbein not only betrayed his integrity as an artist but jeopardized his relationship with Henry by prettifying the portrait? It seems unlikely, for he continued in high favour with the king. A possible explanation, which incidentally throws additional light on Henry's nature, is his brutal remark to Cromwell after the wedding night when the Secretary anxiously asked him if he liked the lady better: 'Nay my lord, much worse for by her breasts and belly she should be no maid; which when I felt them, strake me so to the heart that I had neither will nor courage to prove the rest'. Holbein had been commissioned to provide a portrait, not a figure painting and the unfortunate Anne, though only twenty-five years old, apparently possessed a figure which did not appeal to the fastidious Bluff King Hal with his stinking, ulcerous leg, his bad breath and pendulous breasts and paunch. It was only one factor in Cromwell's downfall, but it proved decisive, for the duke of Norfolk had one additional, devastating weapon in his armoury: his plump, vivacious, nineteen-year-old niece Katherine Howard.

Cromwell's reaction to finding himself in the Tower was precisely the same as his victims: stunned disbelief, followed by terror, then a kind of resignation. He had one further task to perform for his king: providing evidence that would enable the ill-fated marriage to be dissolved. He fairly tumbled over himself to do so, scribbling down details that enabled parliament to declare that there had never been a marriage. At the end of the letter he added, 'Written at the Tower, this Wednesday the last of June with the heavy heart and trembling hand of your highness's most heavy and most miserable and poor slave, Thomas Crumwell'. Then this man, who had never felt mercy, was impelled to scrawl a post-script that not simply pleaded but grovelled: 'Most gracious prince, I cry for mercy, mercy, mercy'.

Cromwell was executed on 28 July 1540. Some accounts record that Tyburn was the place of execution, as befitting Cromwell's common origins. But the fact that his body joined those of his victims in St Peter ad Vincula argues that he was accorded the dubious privilege of dying on Tower Hill, for he was, after all, now an earl of Essex. Unfortunately for him, he possessed almost no neck: even more unfortunately, the axeman was either drunk or nervous and 'ill-favouredly performed his office'.

Regarding the brief but hectic career of Katherine Howard, Henry's fifth wife, one is irresistibly reminded of those Italian peasants who live on the slopes of Mount Vesuvius, perfectly aware that it can wipe them out in moments, prepared to accept the distant risk for the present advantage and in any case convinced that it won't happen to them. There is, perhaps, some excuse for Katherine's blindness. Brought up in a lascivious household where copulation seems to have been the main recreation and deception the norm of conduct, barely nineteen years old when she married: young, vivacious, not very intelligent, she was convinced that she held the king in the strongest of bonds, the sexual. And Henry was besotted with his Kate, his 'rose without a thorn', showering her with jewels, toying with her in public as with some treasured bauble, enjoying her shapely little body to the fullest extent of his declining powers.

All this would naturally make Katherine carry optimism to its ultimate, and fatal conclusion. But her chief lady-in-waiting, Lady Rochford, really ought to have known better. For Lady Rochford was the widow of Anne Boleyn's brother and had heard very clearly the swish and thud of the axe. But instead of restraining

Katherine (Catharine) Howard, third wife of Henry VIII

the silly girl who happened to be the present queen of England, Lady Rochford acted as active bawd, arranging assignations for Katherine's lovers until the inevitable end.

Katherine died well. Grief, perhaps, acted as an anodyne for her, for she had seen the heads of Francis Dereham and Thomas Culpepper on London Bridge as she passed underneath on the way

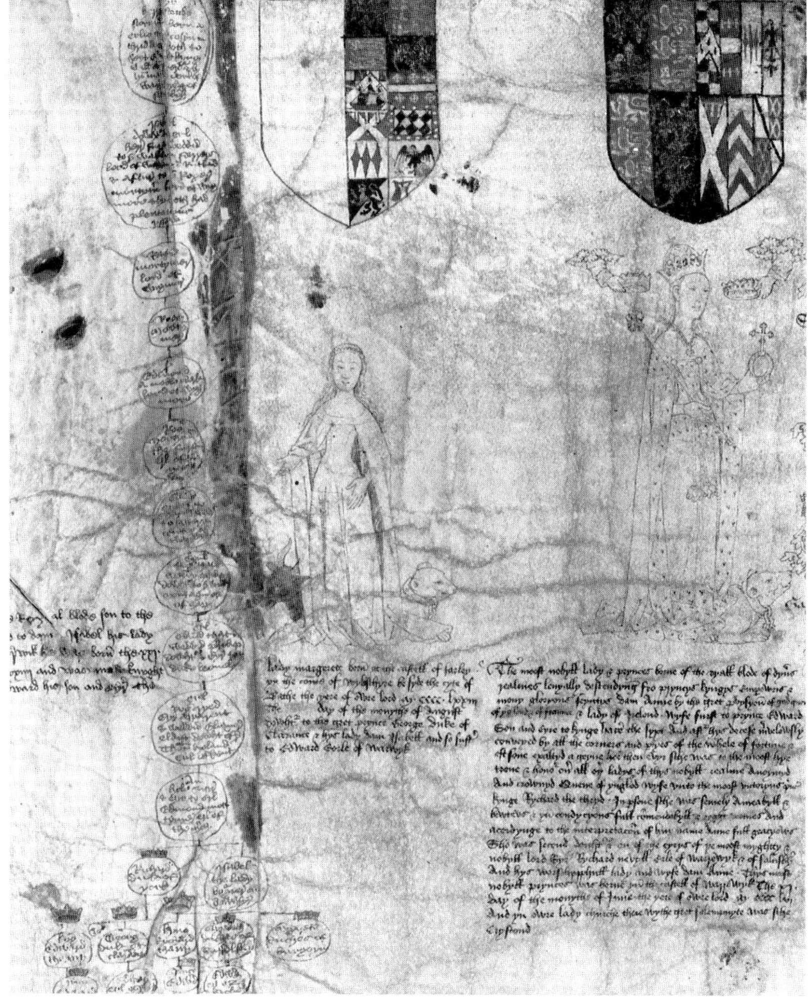

Margaret Pole, countess of Salisbury: the last of the Plantagenets (she is the figure *without* the crown)

to the Tower. Nor, at the end, did she pronounce the customary bland speech with its routine compliments to the king but said forthrightly, 'I die a queen, but I would rather die the wife of Culpepper'. Lady Rochford, on the other hand, seems to have gone off her head with terror and was virtually carried to the scaffold and beheaded in a state of semi-consciousness.

So the bloody tale goes on, the Tower faithfully reflecting conditions in the outside world as England went through its convulsions during its transit from a medieval to a Renaissance, from a Catholic to a Protestant, from an anarchic to a monarchic, society. Some of the victims were dynastic threats, as with the foolish Henry Howard, earl of Surrey, who quartered the royal arms with his own and paid the penalty. Some were idealists, like Robert Aske, who accepted the king's word and helped to disband those Yorkshire rebels who took part in the Pilgrimage of Grace and was hanged in chains for his naïvety. At least two hundred other prisoners from that ill-fated rebellion were executed, some by fire, some by axe.

Margaret Pole, countess of Salisbury, was seventy years old and so, one would have thought, would have died in her bed. But she was the last, the very last, of that Plantagenet dynasty which had been overthrown by the Tudors and was better out of the way. She declined to place her head on the block, spiritedly declaring that she was no traitor. Legend, embellishing as ever, turned that courageous defiance into a macabre story of the executioner pursuing the shrieking woman round and round the scaffold, striking at her with his axe – an inherently improbable story that is occasionally recounted with relish by some of the Tower guides. Certainly there is no need to exaggerate the horrors of the closing years of Bluff King Hal, for the reality is enough to sate any taste for melodrama. There is a certain satisfaction in observing that yet another of the predators finished up as victim when the duke of Norfolk who had presided over the death sentences of his nieces, who had engineered the death of Cromwell and many others, found himself in the Tower under threat of death. But the old fox escaped at last, for the king died the very night before the axe was due to sever Norfolk's stringy neck and he was overlooked in the chaos attending the succession of yet another boy king and by the time his sentence came up for review the paroxysms of violence were gradually dying down.

But the throne of England needed the blood of one more, innocent, victim before it could become stabilized.

Chapter V
The Struggle for Power

The centre of the painting is dominated by a beautiful young woman, dressed in gleaming white satin, kneeling before a solid, plain wooden object. An elderly, distinguished-looking man has his arms tenderly around her and seems to be whispering something to her. Behind her, two richly dressed, slightly older women display grief so intense that one of them has apparently fainted. The eye instinctively travels to the right-hand side of the picture where is standing a tall, strong man of middle years with a handsome, if rugged, face. On his left shoulder is a badge bearing the royal cypher; a coil of rope hangs from his belt and his left hand has begun to reach for a massive axe. His expression, as he glances towards the central figure, is one neither of pity nor of anger but simply the concentrated frown of a craftsman anxious that everything should go well. He is the headsman, the young woman in white is the seventeen-year-old Lady Jane Grey and the occasion is her executed as pictured by the Frenchman, Delaroche, in 1834, creating the archetypal, romantic picture of an 'execution in the Tower'.

Apart from the architectural background and the meagre amount of straw on the scaffold – it was usually necessary to spread masses of sawdust to absorb the great quantities of blood pumped out by the still beating heart – Delaroche's painting is historically accurate. The elderly man is Lord Clinton, who had been Constable of the Tower during the nine-days' reign of Jane the Queen. The executioner did not need the coil of rope to pinion a difficult client. But during the last moments of her life, the young girl's extraordinary calm did momentarily desert her when, blindfolded, she could not find the block and the Constable had to help her.

When Henry VIII died, in January 1547, it would have needed no great perspicuity to predict some such tragedy as the judicial murder of Lady Jane Grey. The new monarch, Edward VI, was a sickly boy not quite ten years of age. So uncertain was his future that his father had actually decreed that, should he die without an heir as seemed only too likely, then the crown should go to his elder halfsister, Mary, then thirty-one years of age and daughter of that rejected queen, Katherine of Aragon, whose divorce had precipitated all the troubles. But Mary was a staunch Catholic while, standing in the wings, were two other young women who, also of the blood royal, nevertheless belonged to that Protestant faith towards which all England was finally turning. They were the fourteen-year-old Elizabeth, daughter of Anne Boleyn, and the sixteen-year-old Jane Grey, granddaughter of Henry VIII's sister, Mary. And, on the distant horizon was yet another young woman, also the granddaughter of another of Henry's sisters, but a Catholic. She was the young woman who would be known to history as Mary, Queen of Scots.

Henry had created a Council of Regency to rule England during his son's minority and the Council, in turn, chose the boy's uncle, Edward Seymour, duke of Somerset to be Lord Protector. But the Council itself was composed of conflicting elements, each fighting to advance its policy. And to add a final ingredient to an already murderous brew was Somerset's bizarre brother, Thomas, who had married Henry VIII's widow, Katherine Parr, and who had gone on to make violent wooing to young Princess Elizabeth after Katherine's death, plotted a *coup d'état* and finished up on the block. Somerset himself twice saw the interior of the Tower as a prisoner. The first occasion was for only a matter of months before the endless jostling for power within the Council brought his allies to the top and in turn brought about his freedom. His powers

The execution of Lady Jane Grey: Delaroche's romantic reconstruction

were, apparently, unaffected for, in gratitude for his treatment by the Tower warders he was able to decree for them a royal livery, forerunner of the livery worn by the Yeomen Warders to this day. His second visit to the Tower proved the last, for his enemies succeeded in bringing him to the block.

The next to emerge out of the struggling mass was John Dudley, earl of Warwick and, later, earl of Northumberland. It is difficult to assess the character of Northumberland. Undoubtedly, he manipulated the young king – that was, in any case, one of the reasons for being on a Council of Regency. Undoubtedly, his machinations brought his old friend Somerset to the block. Undoubtedly, his ravening ambitions for his clan eventually resulted in the tragedy of Lady Jane Grey. But in the last critical hours of the Nine Days' Reign when, in an almost delirious atmosphere of treachery within the Tower, Jane's supposed supporters frantically sought to save their skins at any cost, he conducted himself with dignity. Neither does he seem to have used his role of Protector – for such he was in all but name – for his own, personal advantage. He married his son, Guildford, to the king's young cousin, Lady Jane Grey, and arranged other royal marriage alliances for his other sons. But he also pushed through a measure which would have ended the Regency by enabling young Edward to attain his majority at the age of sixteen instead of eighteen.

But Edward VI died, suddenly, before he attained his majority. Sickly though he was, he had all of his father's stubbornness and self-confidence. One thing he was determined upon was that his Catholic halfsister Mary should, under no circumstances, succeed him whatever their father had decreed. The sudden onset of his illness, coupled with the fact that he was still a minor, made it impossible to arrange a legal transference to the heiress he chose, his cousin Jane Grey. But on his deathbed he commanded, or begged, the members of the Council to respect his dying wish. They agreed, but even the Protestants among them must have done so with deep misgiving.

Edward died on 6 July 1553: Jane the Queen took up residence in the royal apartments of the Tower on 10 July. Her supporters had good reason to choose to make the great fortress her palace for the country was seething with discontent. No matter that the ordinary English person looked upon Mary, with her fanatical Catholicism and passionate love for all things Spanish, with suspicion. She was still the daughter of the 'old Queen', the true heir of Bluff King Hal. Even more important, perhaps, she was a mature woman who knew what she was doing, and not a slip of a girl who would be the pawn of an upstart, scheming family. They were, in fact, quite wrong about Jane's character, but they were not to know that, and as the news spread that a new 'Queen' had been established in the Tower so Mary's support increased. She hurried out of London, set up her standard in the great castle of Framlingham in Suffolk and an army began to gather round her.

Meanwhile, Jane the Queen was thrown into her first battle – with her husband's family. Her selfish young husband demanded the title of 'King' for if his wife were 'Queen' surely he was entitled to no less. Jane refused. She would make him a duke but, in conscience, could do no other. On her second morning in the Tower, while overwhelmed with the official documents produced for her signature, and attempting to give audience, she had to contend with her formidable mother-in-law, the duchess of Northumberland. The duchess was incensed. How dare this slip of a girl, who had been taken from obscurity and given one of the brightest crowns of Europe, refuse so elementary a right to her husband? Jane refused. She did more. In order to make quite clear the distinction between herself, as Queen, and her seventeen-year-old husband as Consort, she decreed that he should take up his residence in the Lieutenant's Lodgings, physically just outside the royal apartments in which she established herself. There the Crown Jewels were brought to her by their Keeper, Lord Winchester, the Crown itself by her proud mother. Jane tried it on briefly, felt its great weight, and put it aside.

Inevitably there is a poignancy around the fate of one so young, beautiful and wholly innocent that must affect the judgement of posterity. But even allowing for that, one comes to the conclusion that in the sixteen-year-old girl was one of the great lost figures of history. Even at that early age she was fluent in French and Italian, knowledgeable in Greek and Latin and probably had a good grasp of Arabic, Hebrew and, it was said, Chaldee. To these she added the expected accomplishments of music and needlework. Above all, she possessed a high – indeed, inflexible – sense of duty and steadfastness to her basic principles. She accepted the Crown reluctantly, because she thought it her duty to do so: she put it aside with relief when it became evident that both law and public sentiment were against her holding it.

Meanwhile, in the world outside the massive walls of the Tower, the tide was turning so strongly in favour of Mary that it was evident that Jane's supporters must put the matter to the test. Northumberland called a meeting of the Council during which it was decided that a military expedition should be launched against Mary. There was one small problem: whoever led that expedition would be unequivocally committing himself. Each member of the Council, including Jane's own father, declined so dangerous an honour. The natural leader of such an expedition was the architect of the whole distrastous affair, the duke of Northumberland himself. Looking round at the veiled expressions of his fellow Councillors, Northumberland must have had the deepest reservations about their loyalty for, before he committed himself, he demanded from each an oath that he was a true man of Jane the Queen. Each gave the oath. 'I pray God it be so. Let us go to dinner,' the duke responded with something less than confidence.

That was on 12 July, just six days after the death of Edward, and two days after Jane's party had taken up residence in the Tower. On 14 July the duke set out for East Anglia at the head of an army which tended to dwindle en route: on the 19th a number of his fellow Councillors discreetly left the Tower, assessed the overall situation and came out in favour of Mary. Among them was Jane's own father, the duke of Suffolk who, under pressure, actually proclaimed Mary as Queen from Tower Hill. He then returned to the Tower, informed Jane that the dream was at an end. As far as she was concerned it had more closely resembled a nightmare and she willingly agreed to move to the Lieutenant's Lodgings, thus leaving the royal apartments to their true occupant, Mary I, Queen of England.

Mary entered London, and promptly took possession of the Tower on 3 August. There then began the game of General Post as Catholics came forward to take the place of Protestants, and those who had backed the right horse emerged to collect their winnings. The first people Mary encountered on entering the Tower were the Catholic prisoners of the old regime, including that veteran survivor, the duke of Norfolk, who had escaped richly deserved

Mary, Queen of England, 'a mercyfull princess'

execution by the timely death of Henry VIII but had languished in prison throughout the disastrous six-years' reign of Henry's Protestant son. He now gained his freedom at the hands of the grateful Catholic queen. Meanwhile, 'Jane the Queen' and her family and immediate supporters endured their own metamorphosis.

Jane was moved from the Lieutenant's Lodgings to the house of the Gentleman Gaoler, Nathaniel Partridge – an honourable and comfortable imprisonment but still, indubitably, an imprisonment. And it is through this move that we get a last, clear, contemporary picture of this extraordinary girl. Partridge had asked if a friend could join them at their common table for dinner: Jane agreed and the friend later recorded the occasion. Jane sat at the head of the table, as befitted her station, but firmly made clear her altered status by insisting that Partridge and his guest should put on their caps, an otherwise unthinkable gesture in the presence of royalty. It seems to have been a relaxed and cheerful dinner party, Jane at that stage having no particular anxiety about her future: she drank to the guest, spoke well of the queen and the talk turned to religious matters. One of the party daringly asked her opinion of the action of the duke of Northumberland. Captured at Cambridge, he had been placed nearby in the Bloody Tower but then, in an apparent attempt to save his neck, had apostasied and turned Catholic. Did her ladyship think that the duke would obtain pardon thereby? For the first time, Jane appeared emotionally stirred. 'Pardon? Wo with him,' she replied vigorously, 'He hath brought me and our stocke in most myserable callamyty and mysery by his exceeding ambicion'. But it was not for the great danger in which Northumberland had placed her that upset Jane, but the fact that he had betrayed his principles. 'I pray God I, nor no frend of myne, dye so.'

Northumberland's apostasy failed to save him. In due course, he met his end on Tower Hill and his headless corpse was to lie near that of his one-time friend and ally in St Peter's ad Vincula. A century later John Stow, the chronicler of London, summed up the first stage of burials in the little church. 'So there lyeth before the High Altar in St Peter's church two dukes, to wit the duke of Somerset and the duke of Northumberland, between two queens [Anne Boleyn and Katherine Howard] all four beheaded'. More, many more were to follow.

During that dinner in the Gentleman Gaoler's house, Jane had remarked of her cousin Mary, 'The Quene's Majesty is a mercyfull princess'. At this stage, her opinion was perfectly justified. Certainly Mary had no ill-feelings towards her. In a letter to the Spanish ambassador she said firmly that Jane 'was never party to, nor did she give her consent to the Duke's intrigues and plots ... My conscience will not permit me to put her to death'. Indeed, the opening of the reign of the woman who would go down in history as Bloody Mary was remarkable for both its religious and for its political tolerance. The Dudley family had tried its best to usurp her position, but the only member of it who suffered the ultimate penalty was the duke of Northumberland. His sons, including Jane's husband Guildford, were lodged in the Beauchamp Tower – where at least one of them showed remarkable skill as a stone carver, creating the most elaborate of all the many graffiti in the Tower. Jane herself continued to reside under the surveillance of Nathaniel Partridge, but waited on by her own maid and with a footman in attendance. She, her husband and two of his brothers were tried at London's Guildhall, found guilty of treason and formally condemned to death, but there is no reason to doubt Mary's word that she could not put her innocent young cousin to death. It was Jane's own foolish father, and an equally foolish courtier, Thomas Wyatt, who precipitated the tragedy and that, in turn, was triggered off by Mary's marriage to Philip of Spain.

Mary's obsession with her mother's country was not shared by the majority of her subjects, even though they had not yet acquired that hatred and fear of 'the Don' which was such a characteristic of Elizabethan England. Nevertheless, after a generation's bloody turmoil, the bulk of English people had no taste for yet more upheaval and Wyatt's rebellion in January 1564 was doomed to failure. It was conducted with sufficient panache, however, to persuade Mary to move to the safety of the Tower, which then experienced the last military engagement of its 500-year-old history, an engagement, moreover, in which artillery was used for the first time. Wyatt's men marched along the south bank of the river, but the heavy bombardment from the Tower's cannons, situated on the White Tower and on St Thomas's Tower, forced them to make an immense circuit, crossing the Thames far to the east at Kingston. Support for Wyatt, lukewarm in any case, had

Wyatt's rebellion, as illustrated in Ainsworth's *Tower of London* (see Bibliography); architecturally accurate, the picture is historically incorrect as the rebels never came near the Tower

totally dwindled by the time he came to Lud Gate where, after a brief skirmish, he was captured. Some 700 men were captured with him, including Jane's father, the duke of Suffolk.

The end of the active rebels was predictable and justifiable. The execution of Jane was as politically unnecessary as it was morally outrageous. Not only had she had nothing whatsoever to do with the rebellion, but any Protestant faction seeking a rallying point would have turned to her cousin, Princess Elizabeth, the daughter of Bluff King Hal, and not to his grandniece, Jane. But the rebellion had shaken Mary's confidence and, urged on by her remorseless Catholic clergy, she entered upon a blood-bath in which Jane and her husband were simply the first to suffer. Compassion, or bigotry, urged Mary to make a last-minute attempt to persuade her cousin to return to the Old Faith. She declined. 'Madam, I am sorry for you', said the priest sent to do the job, 'For I am now sure we shall never meet [in heaven]'. Jane agreed, her quick intelligence turning the question even at this fraught moment: 'I am assured, unless you repent [of your faith] and turn to God you are in a sad and desperate case.' She declined her husband's tearful request for one more meeting before they went to the scaffold, not out of hardness of heart, but because it would upset them both. 'They would meet soon enough in the other world.'

Guildford Dudley was executed, on Tower Hill, his body brought back to be buried in St Peter's. As it happened, Jane was standing at the window of the Gentleman Gaoler's house, which looks inward towards the entrance under the Bloody Tower, and saw her young husband's corpse being brought back, the head casually wrapped in a cloth. Shortly afterwards she followed him, not to Tower Hill, but to that discreet little spot called Tower Green in the heart of the castle, far removed from any sympathetic eyes. She was composed until the very end. But when the blindfold was put on, she became disorientated, desperately searching for the block, whispering 'Where is it? What shall I do?' Compassionately, the Constable placed an arm around the shoulder of the girl who, for nine days had been 'Jane the Queen', and guided her down to the block.

Jane went to her death on 12 February 1554: two months later her twenty-one-year-old cousin, the Princess Elizabeth, was occupying Jane's vacated quarters in the Lieutenant's Lodgings and the shadow of the axe hovered briefly over the young woman whose reign, as Elizabeth I, English people for centuries to come would regard as the Golden Age. Throughout her life, Elizabeth had watched the balance of power oscillating wildly from conservative to radical, from members of the Old Faith to members of the New. At the age of three, she would have heard that her mother's head had been cut off by her father: at the age of fourteen she stood apprehensively on one side while unscrupulous men manipulated her halfbrother, the boy king. In her rural retreat at Hatfield she had heard of the fate of her innocent cousin, Jane. Then had come the most terrible news of all: her halfsister, the queen, herself terrified by Wyatt's rebellion, had had second thoughts: Elizabeth was safest in the Tower. No one knew better than Elizabeth that the road to the Tower was usually one way. In vain, she pleaded with Mary, 'Let conscience move your Highness to take some better way with me than to make me condemned in all men's sight afore my desert be known.' She was taken first to Westminster, then by boat to that ominous watergate generally known as Traitors' Gate. At first she declined to enter by it, spiritedly declaring that she was no traitor and when, eventually, her escort the earl of Sussex persuaded her to disembark, she did so declaring, 'Here landeth as true a subject, being a prisoner, as ever landed at these stairs and before thee, O God, I speak it'.

Elizabeth was taken to the same Lodgings that her mother had occupied eighteen years before and where she was subjected to the closest surveillance and, on Mary's orders, the harshest treatment. Nevertheless, her gaolers were aware of the dangers of being involved in royal affairs, as the earl of Sussex's advice to his fellows makes very clear. 'My lords, let us take heed and do not do more than our commission will bear us out in . . . and further let us consider that she was the king our master's daughter and therefore we should use such dealing [with her] that we may answer it hereafter.' It was very sensible advice, for after two months Mary relented and Elizabeth was removed to the palace of Woodstock in Oxfordshire. Later, when she came to the Tower on the eve of her own coronation, Elizabeth bent down and, patting the earth, said with pardonable satisfaction, 'Some have fallen from being prince of this land to be a prisoner of this place. I am raised from being a prisoner of this place to be a prince of this land'.

With the accession of Elizabeth to the throne of England, the pattern of events within the Tower began to change. Her notorious reluctance to sign death warrants was a source of considerable irritation to her councillors. Men, and women, still passed through the Tower *en route* to the block at Tower Hill, or the noose at Tyburn, but they were, on the whole, rebels against the state: honourable people, for the most part, but intent on forcing through their concept of the right structure for society, whether religious or political, at the cost of stability for the whole of society.

Robert Devereux, earl of Essex, who engineered his own transformation from court favourite to victim

Robert Devereux, earl of Essex, was the only man to have the privilege of a formal execution within the castle itself, and he owed that distinction to an overweening, almost pathological, pride. Robin, Elizabeth called him affectionately: he was one of the curious band of 'courtier-gallants' who hovered round the throne, vying with each other to attract the attention of Gloriana in their ambiguous relationship with that Virgin Queen. Handsome, talented, impulsive Essex had already presumed on that relationship; Elizabeth actually boxed his ears during a quarrel and he had rushed from the royal presence, crying that 'it was an insult which he would not tolerate from her father, much less from a king in petticoats' – not a sentiment likely to endear him to his monarch.

In 1599 he was sent to that politicians' graveyard, Ireland, with wide powers to restore order. Specifically, he was ordered not to return to England until summoned. Nevertheless, he did so, convinced – with considerable justice – that his enemies at court, including Walter Raleigh, were busily undermining his position with the queen. His defiance of a royal order was bad enough but he proceeded to compound the injury by adding insult. Unannounced, he burst into the queen's bedchamber when she had only just risen and was looking every minute of her sixty-two years 'undighted and uncoifed, in the most mortifying disarray, haggard countenance, ere she had time to deliberate in which of her eighty wigs of various hues it would please her to receive the homage of her deceitful courtiers that day'. He was arrested, briefly imprisoned, then punished by having a lucrative monopoly taken from him. Said Elizabeth, 'an ungovernable beast must be stinted of his provender that he may be better managed'. Humiliated, financially crippled, Essex took one more step towards the scaffold. Declaring that Gloriana, with whom it was an act of faith that all men were deeply in love, was simply 'an old woman, crooked both in mind and body', he contacted James VI of Scotland advising him to claim the throne of England.

All this was faithfully retailed to Elizabeth, but curiously she took no active measures until Essex embarked on his greatest folly of all. This handsome, energetic, thirty-three-year-old nobleman was popular with the London mob: like many a celebrity before and after, he mistook a transient, faintly amused interest for deepest loyalty. On Sunday 8 February 1601, he put the matter to the test. Gathering together a force of some 300 supporters – including the earl of Southampton, Shakespeare's later patron, he stormed through the City intent on capturing the Tower. Later, after the collapse of the ludicrous 'rebellion', he claimed that he intended no harm to the queen's royal person, but simply to detach her from the 'traitors' – ie the enemies of Essex – who surrounded her. Armed rebellion was something which even Elizabeth could not overlook, but she did accede to her one-time favourite's request that he should be executed in the privacy of the Tower, and not as part of a show on Tower Hill.

In true Elizabethan manner, Essex dressed and acted the part. He was dressed entirely in black – black velvet cloak, black felt hat, black satin suit – but with a spectacular scarlet waistcoat underneath. The execution was a prolonged affair, with the clergy making the most of their opportunity for public show, urging the victim to a series of prayers both extempore and ritual. That completed, Essex knelt to the block, found it too low and was obliged to prostrate himself fully. The headsman then became worried that his ruff would impede the blow: with admirable patience Essex got to his feet, removed the ruff, then positioned himself again. It took three blows to sever the neck, though, according to an onlooker, the first blow was lethal 'for his bodie never stirred, neither anie part of him more than a stone'. As part of the macabre ritual, the headsman picked up and displayed the head when 'his eyes did open and shut as in the time of his prayer'. The remains then went to join the other victims in the increasingly crowded charnel-house of St Peter ad Vincula.

Elizabeth's sense of personal betrayal is perhaps illustrated by the fact that the earl of Southampton was sentenced merely to imprisonment. He survived, not only to become William Shakespeare's patron, but also to provide the subject for one of the rare contemporary pictures – 'A Prisoner in the Tower'. The romantic-looking young man is depicted in his cell (with a miniature of the Tower in the background) and accompanied by an indignant-looking cat which, it is said, visited him by way of the chimney and enlivened his solitary hours.

Among the privileged spectators at Essex's execution was Walter Raleigh, and even Essex's enemies thought that Raleigh's presence there was in extremely bad taste for he had played no small part in bringing his rival to the block. Under the disapproving glances of his peers, Raleigh removed himself to the White Tower, gazing down with satisfaction at the tragedy being played below. His sense of satisfaction must have been heightened by the fact that he, too, had recently known the interior of the Tower as a prisoner. Posterity might well judge his 'crime' to be, in fact, a gentlemanly act for he had got one of Elizabeth's ladies-in-waiting, Elizabeth Throckmorton, with child and secretly married her. It was a very great mistake for, in return for the favours showered on her courtiers, Gloriana expected total devotion – and that implied sexual as well as political. Incandescent with fury, Elizabeth had thrown him into the Tower as soon as she heard the news.

Walter Raleigh and his son Wat. The boy was destined to die in the ill-fated Orinoco expedition.

The hothouse atmosphere of the Elizabethan court comes out clearly in the grovelling letter which Raleigh wrote to William Cecil, Elizabeth's 'prop and staff', in the sure notice that it would be brought to her attention: 'Even now my heart is cast into the depths of all misery. I, that was wont to behold her riding like Alexander, hunting like Diana, walking like Venus, the gentle wind blowing her fair hair about her pure face like a nymph ...' Gloriana was then in her sixties and, magnificent though she was in character, even the most besotted courtier would have hesitated to describe that raddled face, with the towering red wig and blackened teeth, as belonging to a nymph. But Raleigh, intrepid explorer, consummate seaman and profound scholar though he was, had no hesitation in jumping through hoops to please the Virgin Queen.

On this occasion, Raleigh escaped the Tower with an unblushing act of bribery, making over to Elizabeth his substantial share in a captured treasure ship. However, Elizabeth's rages, though frequent and violent, were not long lasting and he would probably have gained his freedom in due course in any event. His second imprisonment in the Tower, beginning in July 1603 a few months after Elizabeth's death, was at the hands of a far less generous gaoler, King James I. It is difficult to account for James's steady animosity – an animosity preserved over fifteen years – for this essentially honourable man. The actual cause of the imprisonment was yet another plot, the so-called Main Plot whose object was to replace James by his cousin Arabella Stuart. The details are confused: certainly Raleigh's complicity was only peripheral but he, and two aristocrats, Lord Cobham and Lord de Grey, were sentenced to death by a rigged court, the sentence being suspended indefinitely. The three men took up residence in the Tower.

Two years later, in 1605, they were joined by a fourth, the earl of Northumberland, convicted for involvement in yet another conspiracy, the Gunpowder Plot. Northumberland's crime was 'misprison of treason' – concealing knowledge of a plot – and he therefore escaped with imprisonment, while the central figures, including Guy Fawkes, were put to the torture and execution. Raleigh, Cobham, Grey and Northumberland now entered on a most curious way of life which vividly illustrates the fact that a prisoner's life in the Tower did not necessarily, or even usually, approximate to the horror tales which, originally circulated through such publications as Foxe's *Book of Martyrs*, became accepted as standard. Northumberland's accommodation was nothing less than regal. He had, indeed, been lodged at first in the palace itself, but after his vigorous complaints about its by then decayed condition, was moved to the Martin Tower. There he set up a kind of court, personally spending well over £1,000 a year. With his passion for science, he was known as the Wizard Earl, not only conducting his own experiments in alchemy and astrology, but actually engaging three mathematicians to help him in his work. He even rented the Brick Tower, a little further on from the Martin Tower, where his son's education could be pursued under his eye.

The other illustrious prisoners, though they could not match this magnificence, each made himself comfortable in his own way. Lord Cobham, lodged in the Beauchamp Tower, took over an adjacent chamber to house his immense library, while Lord Grey took over St Thomas's Tower. It was, however, the commoner Raleigh who has left the most permanent mark upon the Tower, his lodgings in the Bloody Tower today ranking next only to the Crown Jewels as a visitors' attraction.

Recent work in the Bloody Tower disclosed a number of curious joist holes in the walls. Documentary evidence showed that a second floor had been inserted, turning the naked, austere tower into reasonably comfortable accommodation. In line with the current policy of setting out some of the towers as they would have appeared at a certain period in their long history, Raleigh's lodgings have been furnished much as he would have known them, some of the artefacts on display being directly associated with him (as with the copy of the *History of the World*), others being objects commonly in use at the time. The lower chamber is set out as a living room, the upper as a bedroom. Given the intractable nature of their surroundings, both seem remarkably comfortable.

Raleigh's reaction on being brought to the Tower on the second occasion seems wholly out of keeping with the normal character of this courageous and resourceful man, clear evidence of the now baleful reputation of His Grace's Tower of London. The man who received him, Sir John Peyton, at that time Lieutenant of the Tower, reported 'I never saw so strange a dejected mind as in Sir

Raleigh's lodgings in the Bloody Tower, which he occupied for thirteen years. The upper, bedchamber, floor was specially inserted for him.

Walter Ralegh. I am exceedingly cumbered with him: five or six times a day he sendeth to me in such passions as I see his fortitude is impotent to support his grief'. In his utter despair, Raleigh even attempted suicide, although it seems to have been more of a gesture than a determined attempt, when he grabbed a dinner knife and stabbed at himself.

In due course, he became reconciled to his fate, helped thereto by the fact that his wife was allowed to lodge with him. In 1605, indeed, they christened their second child, Carew, in St Peter ad Vincula, the record of the baby's baptism being one of the few cheerful entries in the register of that melancholy little church. There seems to have been a stream of visitors to the illustrious prisoner: employees from his estate in Wiltshire come to make their report (it was from the estate that the Exchequer drew the £308 allowed him his living expenses): old friends and maritime comrades – even one or two Red Indians he had brought back from Virginia, to whom he was giving instructions in English language and customs.

Also among the many visitors was King James's own son, Prince Henry – an open, upstanding, highly intelligent youth, utterly different from the effeminate young men with whom his father surrounded himself, drawn towards the prisoner in the Bloody Tower as though he were a father figure. Bitterly Henry remarked, 'Only my father would keep such a bird in such a cage'. Raleigh responded generously. It was for young Prince Henry that he began his immense *History of the World*, a study designed to show that kings had a reciprocal responsibility towards their subjects as to present an overall history. Given the circumstances in which it was written, together with the state of historical knowledge of the period, the *History* is astonishingly well balanced and readable, even now that much of its conclusions have been superseded. Raleigh's intention that the mammoth work should be a kind of vade-mecum for the heir to the throne is shown by the fact that he abandoned it, only one third completed, when young Prince Henry died 'of a fever' and England lost a potentially great king.

Raleigh was fortunate in his first two gaolers, John Peyton and, later, Sir George Harvey. With the latter's benign permission, he established a kind of laboratory in an old henhouse in the garden where he seems to have anticipated a nineteenth-century discovery by distilling drinkable water from seawater. In the gardens he grew a variety of herbs, many of them derived from plants he had brought back from the New World. Combining his alchemic and botanical experiments, he produced two famous cordials which were much in demand: Balsam of Guiana (variously described as being compounded of strawberry water, or a disgusting distillation of viper remains) and the famous Great Cordial, composed of over forty herbs mixed with an extraordinary range of ingredients including pearl, coral and antimony.

So the slow years went by. Raleigh and his fellow prisoners suffered a setback when a martinet succeeded the easygoing George Harvey as Lieutenant. Sir William Waad was a career diplomat, a cold, utterly ruthless but efficient man whose prime task at the Tower was to extract the fullest possible confessions from the Gunpowder Plot conspirators confined in the Tower. But he also cast a cold and critical eye on the remarkable laxity of discipline that prevailed within. Northumberland, Raleigh and the rest acted as though they were guests, not prisoners, of the king: ignoring the curfew, visiting each others' quarters, receiving streams of guests. Waad was particularly incensed by Raleigh's habit of strolling along the section of wall which linked the Bloody Tower and the Lieutenant's Lodgings. Known today as Raleigh's Walk, the section overlooks the encircling outer wall so that anyone standing upon can see, and be seen from, the Wharf. Raleigh took full advantage of this to display himself to the increasing number of people who wanted to see the now legendary prisoner in the Tower. Waad also protested that visitors to the Tower had got into the habit of gossiping with Raleigh as he worked in his little garden and, to stop that, a high wall was built around it emphasizing Raleigh's status as prisoner. Inhuman though these measures seem, they were not simply spiteful but an attempt by a responsible officer to discharge his office: the relative ease with which prisoners could escape through a combination of bribery, and incompetence on the part of the warders, was more a characteristic of the Tower than its reputation as a torture-chamber. Waad's reforms proved effective. Northumberland was released after sixteen years due to high influence at court: Grey and Cobham died of natural causes: Raleigh was executed by more or less due process of law.

Raleigh's end echoed that of the Golden Age of Elizabeth of which he was the last survivor, an age curiously compounded of the romantic and the practical, the squalid and the magnificent, the generous and the mean. He left the Tower in March 1616, thirteen years after entering it, on the wildest of wild-goose chases, nothing less than a search for that El Dorado which had haunted the dreams of Europeans ever since the conquest of Central America. James I's hunger for gold proved slightly stronger than his passion for revenge. Raleigh was permitted to make a journey to the Orinoco, in search of that fabulous city which supposedly contained more treasures than all those of the Incas and Aztecs put together, provided the royal exchequer received a substantial portion of the plunder. For plunder it was – or would have been if such a city existed – for Guinea was under the control of Spain, and England and Spain were, supposedly, at peace.

The expedition proved an utter disaster. Not only was El Dorado never found, but Raleigh's force clashed with the Spanish. His only son, Wat, who had spent years with him in the Tower, was killed: the Spaniards, rightly outraged by the incursion into their own colonies, demanded Raleigh's head. He must have known what was in store for him when he landed back at Plymouth, fourteen months after the hopeful departure to the New World. He might have escaped by going to France, but he was an old man now, probably in his sixty-sixth year, in failing health, heartsick, at the end of his quite remarkable resilience. There was no need to stage a full trial yet again: all that was needed was to activate the death sentence passed in 1603 and this avoided the embarrassment of admitting that the raid on the colony of a 'friendly' state was actually authorized by the king. On 27 October 1618, fifteen years after he entered the Tower, he was executed in Palace Yard, Westminster. The last of the 'universal men' of the English Renaissance, as skilled in poetry as in swordsmanship, the poem he wrote in the Tower well sums him up:

What is our life? a play of passion
Our mirth the music of division
Our mothers' wombs the tyring houses be
Where we are dressed for this short comedy,
Heaven the judicious sharp spectator is
That sits and marks still who doth act amiss
Thus march we playing to our latest rest.
Only we die in earnest: that's no jest.

CHAPTER VI
INSIDE THE TOWER

Legend wraps the Tower round: legend seizing on garbled history to embellish it further for the purposes of propaganda, religious or political and, later, to please the palates of a posterity avid for sensation. Despite the uncounted tons of records that accumulated in the Tower over the centuries, great gaps remained in its published history, gaps which were inevitably filled with speculation and outright invention.

It was not until 1830 that the first comprehensive, objective history of the great monument was published. The author was John Bayley and he, drawing upon original material instead of simply retailing legends, provided an authentic source-book from which all subsequent writers have gratefully drawn. But, part topographical guide, and part biographical account of the 'Distinguished Prisoners' which fill most of its pages, Bayley's *History* is written from the outside as it were. Only in our own time has material begun to emerge which, written by or on behalf of actual inmates of the Tower, provides a view of life within it. Two outstanding personal accounts, separated by over a century, and written from the entirely different points of view of a prisoner, and a gaoler, provide a continuous view, in depth, over a period of great change. The prisoner was John Gerard, a Jesuit priest who was imprisoned in 1597 but whose *Autobiography* was not published until 1951. The gaoler was Adam Williamson, Deputy-Lieutenant of the Tower from 1722 to 1747, in whose time the last execution (apart from that of the spy in the Second World War) took place.

Gerard states that he wrote his book, some four or five years after the events it describes, on the orders of his superiors so that it could act as a guide for other Jesuit missionaries about to make the perilous journey through underground England. His style is brisk, sinewy, immensely readable. Vividly he describes the secret landing in Norfolk, then making his way through a country hungry for the blood of him and his kind: the hiding in priests' holes while searchers thumped and swore outside: taking the Sacrament to the people until the inevitable end in the spring of 1594 when he was betrayed and arrested in London. For three years he was held as a prisoner in the Clink in Southwark, again and again questioned as to his movements and the identity of those who helped him until, on 12 April 1597, he was removed to the Tower.

The Governor, Berkeley, took him personally to the Salt Tower and there specifically placed him in the care of a warder called Bennett. Prisoner and warder were to develop one of those curiously close relationships which frequently did develop between bored (and underpaid) warder and a lively prisoner with access to cash. Gerard slept well that first night on straw considerately spread by Bennett and on the following morning performed that routine which all prisoners perform – exploring his confined environment. The cell had been earlier occupied by a prisoner whom Gerard and other Catholics regarded as a saint – Father Henry Walpole – and, to Gerard's delight, he found that Walpole had followed the Tower tradition and carved his name in large, deep letters on the wall. (They are still to be seen in the Salt Tower.)

This cell, with its relic of the tortured martyr, became a holy place to Gerard. He protested against being moved, for security reasons, to the upper floor, but the kindly Bennett allowed him to come down and say his prayers in the sanctified cell. He and Bennett also conducted negotiations for a bed. Gerard confirms that prisoners were allowed to introduce furniture into their 'lodgings' on the understanding that it became the property of the

Lieutenant when they left the Tower – one of the mosaic of 'perks' which financed the running of the castle as a prison.

Bennett got the bed from some friends of Gerard's outside the Tower who, Gerard said, told him 'to come and ask them for whatever I needed: he only had to bring a note signed by me. Then they put some money in his hands and begged him to treat me well'. Reading this account, it becomes only too clear why escape from the Tower was relatively easy. Two-way traffic between prisoners and their allies outside the Tower, with a warder as go-between and obviously paid for his trouble, was a commonplace.

On the third day of Gerard's imprisonment, Bennett came to his cell 'looking sorry for himself'. The Lords Commissioners had arrived and Gerard's presence was needed for their enquiry. Bennett accompanied him to the Lieutenant's Lodgings where a five-man Commission – including Francis Bacon – were waiting to interrogate him. That interrogation went the way with which he had become only too familiar over the past three years, with the Commissioners insisting that his mission to England was political and Gerard insisting that it was purely religious. 'They then asked me about the letters I had recently received from abroad and I realised for the first time why I had been removed to the Tower': the Commission believed the letters to be of political importance.

The incident illustrates the dilemma in which both sides found themselves. Gerard and his fellow-Catholics undoubtedly sincerely believed that their objective was purely religious but, as that objective involved the excommunication – in fact outlawry – of the reigning queen of England and the overturning of the country's entire political structure, there is small wonder that the authorities regarded their actions as inimical. Gerard refusing to confess, a warrant was drawn up for his torture. Curiously pedantic, he notes, 'I saw that the warrant was properly made out and signed'.

His description of what happened next is one of the very few authentic descriptions of torture in the Tower. The man in charge was Waad – that same man whom Raleigh would describe as 'that beast Waad' when he was promoted to Governor. The actual executioner 'was a well-built man whom Waad called Master of Torture. He was Master of Artillery. Waad gave him this title to terrorise me'. Gerard describes the 'torture chamber' as being underground, dark and vast. In fact, it was simply the ground floor of the White Tower and though Gerard was shown a number of horrific instruments his own torture was brutally simple and effective: he was manacled and hung from a wooden post. 'A gripping pain came over me. It was worst in my chest and belly, my hands and arms. All the blood in my body seemed to rush up into my arms and hands and I thought that blood was oozing out from the ends of my fingers and the pores of my skin.' He hung there for hours. Bennett was among those who remained with him, wiping the perspiration from his face, urging him to confess. Waad returned about four o'clock, asking Gerard if he were now prepared to obey the Commission. Gerard declined. 'In a rage, Waad turned his back on me and strode out of the room, shouting angrily in a loud voice, "Then hang there till you rot off the pillar".' He was taken down later that evening, but hung again on the two following days. According to his own account, the Governor protested against the cruelty and actually resigned his office. Whether for this reason, or because the Commissioners simply despaired of breaking Gerard, the torture was stopped after three days.

Back in his cell he became the object of solicitude on the part of Bennett, who cut up his food for him for many days until his swollen hands returned to normal. The naïve warder now became the unwitting instrument for Gerard's escape. The Salt Tower is on the south-east corner of the inner curtain wall with the thoroughfare now known as Walter Lane between it and the outer walls. Almost opposite, however, is the Cradle Tower, much lower in height than the Salt Tower and originally built to house an ingenious device – the 'cradle' which allowed boats to be hoisted up direct from the river. Imprisoned in this tower was another captive, Arden, who was actually under sentence of death. Gerard realized that escape from this tower would be a relatively simple matter without outside help. At first he tried bribing Bennett with the offer of 1,000 florins down and 100 florins a year for life, but the warder declined even this colossal bribe, saying he would be an outlaw for the rest of his life.

Gerard thereafter tried subterfuge. Bennett was willing to carry messages, and even to allow his prisoner to visit Arden in the Cradle Tower. At first, Gerard painstakingly wrote his messages in invisible ink, using orange juice for the purpose but, after realizing that the unfortunate warder could not read, he communicated openly.

The escape was planned for the night of 8 September, the arrangement being that Gerard should spend the night with Arden. His friends outside would approach under the cover of darkness and, tying up on the wharf below the Cradle Tower, throw up a rope. The first attempt was a failure, the fierce current under London Bridge nearly sinking the would-be rescuers' boat. The second attempt succeeded, although Gerard nearly crashed in the moat, the pain in his still swollen hands being so great that he had difficulty holding on to the rope. He left three letters, the first to Bennett – 'the purpose of the letter was to put him less at fault in case he was imprisoned for our escape': the other two letters, to the Lieutenant and the Lords of the Council respectively, also stressing that no Tower official had taken part in the escape.

The extraordinarily casual and confused manner in which prisoners were guarded is brought out clearly in Williamson's diary. A meticulous disciplinarian, he tried to bring some order into the system shortly after being appointed Lieutenant of the Tower in 1722: 'All the doors of Warders houses were numbered by figures being painted on them so that hereafter it will be known where prisoners were lodged'. The inescapable implication is that, before this obvious means of control was introduced, no one person knew who was staying where. Later he recorded how a particularly troublesome prisoner was shifted from warder to warder: 'Plunket the Prisoner being too great a trouble to any one warder to have him allwais Lodg'd in his house, they petitioned to have turn about for one year at each Warder's house. I ordered 'em to cast lots and Settl'd the allowance he was to make 'em out of the 5 shillings ye day which the King allowed him: vizt ten pound p. an for his Lodging and 1s a day for the Warder's attendance'.

Born in 1676, Lieutenant-General Adam Williamson was forty-six years of age when he was appointed to the Tower. A professional soldier who enjoyed the personal favour of George II, he was a bigoted, but upright and honest man, discharging his frequently unpleasant tasks to the letter, but also with what compassion the regulations allowed. He recorded once, 'I determined never to see the blood of a prisoner shed before me', and he kept that vow. He held his office for twenty-five years, usually spending the summer months at his home in Berkshire, though prepared to return at a moment's notice if necessary. Thus when riots broke out among the Irish in nearby Spitalfields, 'The first news of this disturbance brought me Post to Towne'. In the last years of his appointment, as his health deteriorated, he received permission to live in Islington and so escape the miasma arising from the stinking moat which terminated many a life within the Tower. Throughout that quarter century he monitored the life of the Tower, copiously recording his observations, whether it were dining with the Constable, the earl of Leicester, in his house in what is now Leicester Square, preparing for the execution of the Scottish rebel lords, or disciplining the warders.

'The Constable was pleased to give me leave to live in his house on the Parade which I furnished handsomely and at great expence', he records. The 'house on the Parade' was that which is today known as the Queen's House, the residence of the current Governor. Williamson would have appeared to have enjoyed considerably more privacy than the present resident for where, today, there is simply a stretch of open lawn separated from the public only by a chain-link Williamson enjoyed a quite extensive garden, the same in which Raleigh walked and where Williamson now planted vines, pears and 'in the Ditch behind the Bridge seven young Elder trees in order to have berries for making wine'.

Williamson's pedantic notes provide a clear picture of the bewildering mosaic of customs, prize money, tips, rents, fees and straightforward perks (which indeed he frequently refers to quite frankly as 'perquisites') which paid for the everyday running of the castle as a prison. First and foremost were the allowances which the government made for the subsistence of a prisoner. Gerard had made the point that such allowances were paid on a scale according to social position, which he thought quite wrong, and Williamson confirms this. The scale in his day was: £2 per week for a commoner, £2 4s 5d for a bishop, £2 13s 4d for an archbishop. English peers were classed at the same rate as an archbishop, whereas Scots or Irish peers were downgraded to bishops. Prisoners contracted with Williamson at so much a week for their subsistence, out of which he made a profit. That profit seems to have been decidedly slender, judging by the bitter letter he wrote to the Constable shortly before his retirement. The warders had been complaining that their own allowance of a shilling a week was not enough and demanded more, complaining to the Constable. 'My Lord,' wrote poor Williamson, 'here is the strongest reason why I should give them no more. My goods are all spoild, so is the Table Linnen: my pewter lost or embezzled, sheets ruined: two bottles of best port allowed them daily besides strong beer . . .'

There was an additonal source of income, in the traditional 'presents' made by a departing prisoner. When Lord Orrerey was discharged in 1722 Williamson noted sourly, 'This poor-spirited Lord did not make the least present to the Officers on going out.' On the other hand, when the earl of Macclesfield was discharged after paying a massive fine of £3,000 Williamson observed, 'In regard, his fine was so heavy that I thought him an honest man and hardly dealt with: I did not take one farthing from him'. He frankly records another, somewhat dubious means of income: 'We look on the goods of those committed for High Treason, and left in the Tower after the death of the Prisoner, as the perquisite of the Commanding officer of the Tower'. But he was prepared to waive his claim. When the troublesome John Plunket died after an operation, he allowed Plunket's nephew to have his 'books, money and clothes' because they were of small value.

The Tower's proximity to Britain's largest port allowed the garrison to levy a kind of freelance customs duty on ships entering it. This was done in the same curiously casual, *ad hoc*, basis as was the custodianship of prisoners. Between 1605 and 1619 the self-styled Water Poet, William Taylor, held the important-sounding post of Keeper of the Tower Bottles. Taylor was, to put it at its kindest, a fixer. Misliking the strenuous life as a waterman, he had turned his hand to anything that would yield a relatively honest penny – knocking out doggerel verse, writing pamphlets, organizing pageants. Somehow he got himself appointed Bottle Keeper which gave him the right to levy a wine tax on all ships carrying wine. In his doggerel poem 'Farewell to the Tower Bottles' he reveals that there were two leather bottles, holding some six gallons between them, which he filled on board ship, placing the contents in the Lieutenant's cellar – after undoubtedly making a substantial deduction for his own purposes. Regretfully,

The port of London with the Tower at its heart, 1819

Williamson records the ending of the custom: 'I find that formerly the Lieutenant of the Tower had a Patant by which he took custom of Wine, Oysters and other Victuals passing by the Tower. The tradition was at my coming to the Tower, strong'. But Parliament, he said, had decreed its ending. Nevertheless, the Tower still retained the curious right of claiming any cattle or carts which fell into the river from London Bridge.

The tipping of the warders by visitors and tourists generally was a time-honoured custom – certainly since the time of Thomas Platter who, in 1599, complained that his party had been mulcted no less than eight times during their visit. The warders, it would seem, had no compunction about putting pressure on visitors and in 1724 an order went out to them that 'they are to attend on Strangers and to take money of those who are inclined to give it to them – but to stop or force no man to it'. Tips were supposed to go into a common pool. When Williamson learned that a visitor had given a warder the very handsome sum of three guineas and the man had not declared it, he suspended the warder 'and ordered him to be a prisoner at his lodgings for not letting his brother warders know it, and endeavouring to keep it a secret'. Despite the warders' frequent complaints about their level of pay, they seem to have lived very well. Williamson records the death of at least four of them from gluttony ('eating of flesh meat night and noon'), drink and apoplexy generally. Apart from tips and official pay, the warders had other means of boosting income. Williamson records that 'When Mother Thomas, an old Drunken Woman who kept the Warder's Sutling [provisions] House by the guard room at the Wharf bridge, dyed and was so poor that her effects could but bury her' the warders claimed the rent of the house. Curiously, despite the privilege of a handsome livery which Protector Somerset had granted their predecessors, the Yeomen Warders seemed indifferent to their appearance and Williamson had to criticize them for it: 'Seeing the Warders with their coats open under which appeared westcoats of Vareous colours, black, browns, grays etc, I persuaded 'em to make handsome Lace vests of their old coats to appear in when on Duty, or called to appear at Coronation etc.'

It was during Williamson's tenure of office that the very last executions took place on Tower Hill, that of the rebel Scottish lords Balmerino, Kilmarnock and Lovat. The event aroused tremendous interest and copious notes from outside sources and these, together with Williamson's own detailed account, provide a clear picture of this moment of historical change. Balmerino and Kilmarnock were tried first. That old gossip, Horace Walpole, was as ever, minutely informed. 'Old Balmerino keeps up his spirits to the same pitch of gaiety', he wrote to a friend. 'In the cell at Westminster he showed Kilmarnock how he must lay his head – bid him not to wince lest the stroke should cut his skull or his shoulders, and advised him to bite his lips. As they were to return [to the Tower] he begged that they might have another bottle together as they should never meet any more till – and then pointed to his neck. At getting into the coach he said to the gaoler "Take care, or you will break my shins with this damned axe".'

Back at the Tower, on the morning of 11 August, Williamson received from the Treasury Solicitor the customary seal in yellow wax authorizing him to deliver up the bodies of Kilmarnock and Balmerino to the Sheriffs of London 'at the usual place for execution on Monday next'. On the 17th, he and the Sheriffs set their watches and agreed that the handover should take place at precisely 10am. The Gentleman Gaoler had begged Williamson's permission to use part of the surrounding scaffolding and sheds as grandstands for spectators. Williamson agreed 'provided he took it as a favour from me and not as a right', and the Gaoler made a handsome profit.

As soon as the prisoners had vacated their cells 'I had the doors lockt after them and the keys given to me, that if any Valluable thing was left in them I might secure it as My Perquisite'. An impressive procession then formed up. Four warders led the way, followed by Williamson, then Kilmarnock with the Tower Major (the officer responsible for military matters). Two chaplains came after, followed by Balmerino with the Gentleman Gaoler. Thirty soldiers of the garrison divided into two companies with two hearses carrying the two coffins in between, brought up the rear. At the gate, the handover to the Sheriffs duly took place. Williamson records: 'I stayed in the Tower, but ordered the Officer who attended the prisoners and their herses, as soon as they arrived at the scaffold to let the Undertaker take the coffins out of the herses and lay them together on the stage or scaffold and after the execution to lay the bodys in the coffins . . . and conduct them back in the Tower for their immediate interment in the Tower Chap le'.

Despite his vow 'never to see the blood of a prisoner shed' Williamson took pains to inform himself as to what happened on the scaffold. Both lords had carefully checked that the plates for their coffins provided correct biographical information, and Kilmarnock had –

> . . . ordered one of his Warders to attend him as his Vallet de Chambre, and to keep down the body from struggling or violent convulsive motion, but it only bounced backward on the separation of the head and lay on its back, with very little motion. It is probable that whenever the head is severd from the body at one Stroke it will alwais give that convulsive bounce or spring. Lord Balmerino's fate was otherwise, for tho he was a resolute Jacobite and seemed to have more than ordinary courage, and indifference to death, yet when he layd his head on the block it is sayd by those on the scaffold that when he made his own signal for decollation, he withdrew his body, so that he had three cuts with the Axe before his head was severed and that the by Standers were forc'd to hold his body and head to the

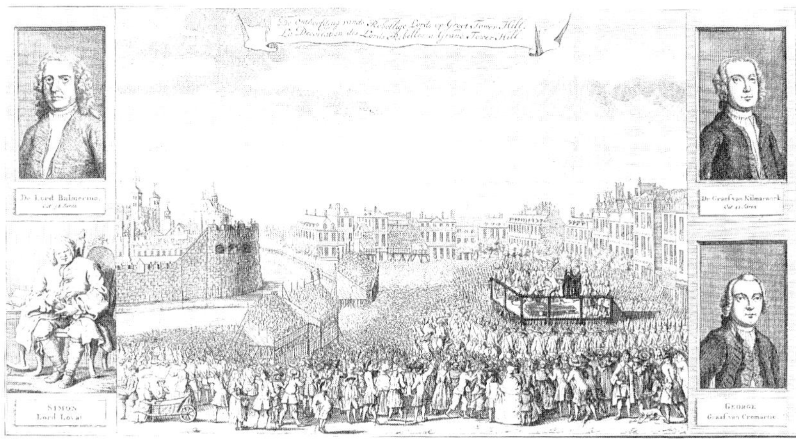

A Dutch version of the execution of the Scottish rebel lords in 1746. Apart from the absence of All Hallows Church, this is a reasonably accurate view of Tower Hill in the eighteenth century.

> block while the Seperation was making. After all was over and I had dined I sent my servants with the Keys to open their Prisons and bring all their effects to me as of right I aught, but being little worth and no plate or things of dignity, I gave them all to the Warders.

Eight months later, on 3 April 1747, Simon Fraser, Lord Lovat, became the last person in history to be executed on Tower Hill, 400 years after the first.

Lord Lovat is almost universally criticized. Horace Walpole, writing to Horace Mann, said, 'I did not think it possible to feel so little as I did at so melancholy a spectacle but tyranny and villainy, wound up with bufoonery, took off all the edge of concern'. On his capture, Lovat abjectly pleaded for mercy from Butcher Cumberland: 'I often carried your Royal Highness in my arms ... I can do more service to the King than the destroying a hundred such old and infirm men like me past 70'. He even offered to trade in his son.

But it is difficult not to feel a touch of admiration for the old rogue in his last days, for he carried himself off well. Hogarth saw him when he was being brought to London and made that famous sketch of him counting the rebels on his fingers and leering at the spectators. It says how much interest there was in this, the last of the Scottish lords, that the canny Hogarth made £12 a day selling engravings of his painting. On the way back to the Tower after Lovat had been condemned at Westminster, a crone stuck her head into his coach and said gleefully, 'You ugly old dog, don't you think you will have that frightful head cut off?' He replied: 'You ugly old bitch, I believe I shall'.

The crowds at his execution were unprecedented, greater even than for the execution of the earl of Stafford, Charles I's hated counsellor, almost exactly a century earlier. One of the hastily erected stands near the scaffold collapsed, killing a number of the

Below Simon Fraser, Lord Lovat, one of the rebel lords

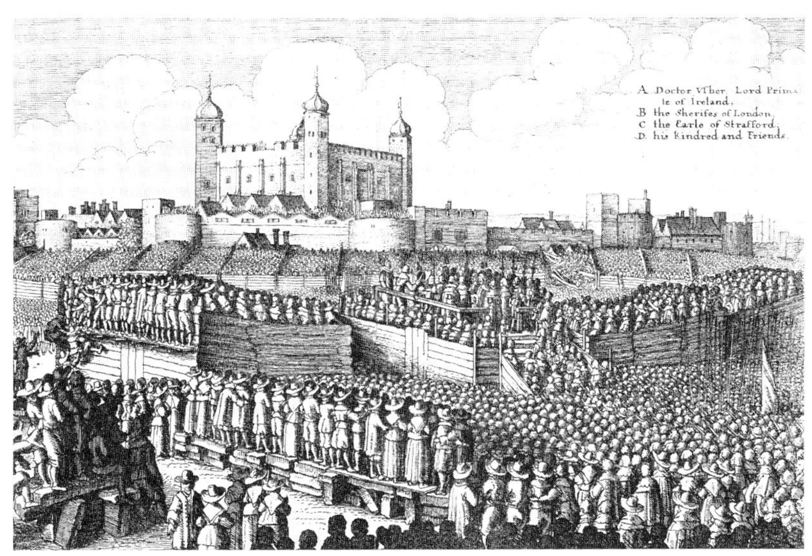

Tower Hill in the seventeenth century: the execution of the earl of Strafford in 1641. Compare with that opposite.

would-be spectators, occasioning Lovat's delight – 'the more mischeif the more sport'. As he was helped up the scaffold he looked round mockingly at the vast sea of faces: 'God save us. Why should there be such a bustle about taking off an old grey head that needs cannot go up three steps without three bodies to support it.' On the scaffold he placed spectacles upon his nose and carefully read the identifying plate upon his coffin. Then, satisfied and quite calm, he yielded himself up to the headsman.

Williamson's diary ends with the bald statement, dated 3 April, that 'The order came for delivering [Lord Lovat] to the sheriffs of London and Midx for execution on Thursday 9th'. He survived the last victim on Tower Hill only by nine months. It is probable, indeed, that the anxieties attending the custody of these illustrious prisoners undermined a health already weakened by living conditions in the Tower. He died in 1748, and though he had arranged to be buried alongside his beloved first wife, Catherine, in the Tower's chapel of St Peter ad Vincula he was laid to rest – probably at his second wife's injunction – near his Berkshire home.

> In truth there is no sadder place on earth than this little cemetery. Death is there not associated, as in Westminster and St Paul's, with genius and virtue and with imperishable renown: nor, as in our humblest churches and churchyards, with everything that is most endearing in social and domestic charities; but with whatever is darkest in human nature and human destiny; with the savage triumph of implacable enemies; with the inconstancy, the ingratitude, the cowardice of friends; with all the miseries of fallen greatness and blighted fame. Thither have been carried through successive ages, by the rude hands of gaolers, without one mourner following, the bleeding relics of men who had been the captains of armies, the leaders of parties, the oracles of senates and ornaments of courts.

Lord Macaulay's celebrated threnody on the chapel of St Peter, written in 1848, was prompted by the changes made in the

'In truth there is no sadder place on earth'; the nave of St Peter ad Vincula in 1971, before the chapel's recent rearrangement

eighteenth century 'which has transformed this interesting little church into the likeness of a meeting house in a manufacturing town'. A contemporary illustration bears out his criticism for the beautiful ceiling of Spanish chestnut has been hidden by a false plaster ceiling, and a gallery and cumbersome box pews hide the chapel's elegant proportions. There was little interest in a decaying Gothic chapel, however, and nearly a quarter of a century was to pass before the condition of St Peter's attracted the attention of the highest person in the land as the result of a macabre discovery.

In 1870, gravediggers opening up a grave for the late Constable, Sir John Fox Burgoyne, found themselves digging through a skeleton whose head was detached from its body. Later investigation showed that the skeleton was that of John Dudley, duke of Northumberland, whose ambitions had led to the brief and tragic reign of Lady Jane Grey. Indications were that many other skeletons, some buried barely two feet deep, lay under the uneven floor of the nave. The fact was reported to Queen Victoria who, shocked, ordered that a full investigation of the graves be made. A committee came into being in 1876 and its report unfolded a remarkable story. The little church was crammed with human remains, probably numbering some hundreds. Most were ordinary citizens of the vicinity, for the nave and churchyard were used as a parish burial ground, but scattered among them, frequently without identification, were the remains of the historic persons known to have been buried there after execution.

One of the early discoveries in the chancel was the grave of an otherwise unknown woman called Hannah Beresford. These remains were found at a considerable depth but above them and to one side were the bones and skull of another woman, neatly piled together. A medical member of the committee – Dr Frederic Mouat – examined the bones and came to the conclusion that they were 'all consistent with the published descriptions of the Queen [Anne Boleyn] and the bones of the skull might well belong to the person [Anne Boleyn] portrayed by the painting by Holbein'. Nearby, another female skeleton was discovered in approximately the position believed to have been occupied by the remains of Katherine Howard. Mouat dismissed the idea for the bones discovered 'were those of a woman probably forty years of age of larger frame than Katherine Howard'. Who this person was, and why she was buried in a relatively important part of the church, remained unknown.

So the macabre treasure hunt went on. The skeleton of James, duke of Monmouth, was found in an isolated position in front of the high altar. Near him, but nearly a foot deeper was the skeleton of a big man with the head lying north-east and the feet south-west. The man, whoever he was, had been buried some time after the burial of the seventy-year-old countess of Salisbury – murdered like so many of the church's occupants by Henry VIII and buried in 1541 – and the man's skeleton had probably been disturbed during the burial of the notorious Judge Jeffreys. By one of the ironies of history Jeffreys was buried near the body of the duke of Monmouth, whose followers Jeffreys persecuted so vigorously, but was afterwards removed to a church in the City. The bodies of the three Scottish lords, Balmerino, Kilmarnock and Lovat, were discovered still in their coffins: the name plates which each had inspected with such care were removed and placed on the wall while the remains were transferred to the crypt.

Not all the Tower's victims finished up in the chapel: the earl of Surrey, beheaded in 1546 for his presumption in quartering the royal arms with his own, was first buried in All Hallows then removed to the family seat of Framlingham in Suffolk: Walter Raleigh was buried in St Margaret's, Westminster, the head being embalmed and removed by his wife: the earl of Stafford finished up in Yorkshire and Archbishop Laud, after temporarily resting in All Hallows was moved to St John's College, Oxford. Altogether, thirty-four historic figures were identified in the chapel, their names inscribed on a brass plate still to be seen on the south wall. The chancel was paved with handsome marble slabs and the approximate situation of the fifteen bodies buried beneath it (among them Anne Boleyn, Jane Grey and her husband and Katherine Howard) were marked with their respective coats of arms.

The fashionable architect, John Salvin, restored the chapel according to the Gothic taste of the day which, though a decided improvement on the earlier 'restorations', still obscured the Tudor origins of the chapel. In 1970, however, a major work of restoration has returned the chapel of St Peter ad Vincula to its original appearance. Its curious name – St Peter in Chains – while

The Salt Tower exterior, taken from the wall walk. John Gerard's cell (see page 73) was behind the window visible on the left.

it may seem particularly appropriate for the grimmest period of the Tower's history – is derived from a church of the same name in Rome where are displayed what purports to be the chains that secured St Peter during his imprisonment. Today, access to the beautiful and poignant little chapel is very closely controlled, visitors permitted to enter it only in guided groups.

On 17 November 1796, the Reverend John Brand, Secretary to the Society of Antiquaries, read a paper to his colleagues:

> There is a room in Beauchamp's Tower, in the Tower of London, anciently the place of confinement for state prisoners, and which has lately been converted into a mess-room for the officers of the garrison there. On this alteration being made a great number of inscriptions were discovered on the walls of the room which probably have, for the most part, been made with nails and are all of them, it should seem, the undoubted

autographs, at different times, of the several illustrious and unfortunate tenants of this once dreary mansion.

In that manner was brought to the public what must be the most remarkable range of spontaneous graffiti in the world. There are, of course, far older ones for the graffiti scratched by tourists in the Nile valley must antedate these by a millenium and more. But in their details (and some of the Tower's graffiti are works of art) and in the poignant information they convey, they are unique.

The human urge to achieve immortality by scratching marks on a wall has two elements: the name or initials of the graffiti-ist and the date. Using these one can, very roughly, relate the prisoner and his graffiti to events in the outside world. Thus the first main set in the Tower of London, dated around 1537, relate to that upheaval during Henry VIII's reign known as the Pilgrimage of Grace, probably sparked off by the suppression of the monasteries. Adam Sedbar, abbot of Jervaulx in Yorkshire, carved his name, office and the date in the Beauchamp Tower before being led out to execution. Wyatt's rebellion, which brought Lady Jane Grey to the block, produced its own crop.

Among the English inscriptions is one Italian. The Salt Tower contains doggerel verse signed 'Giovanni Battista Castiglione, 1556': almost certainly he was the Italian tutor of Princess Elizabeth, thrown into the tower as a result of Queen Mary's suspicions of her halfsister. Most of the inscriptions are simple names crudely carved, like that of Henry Walpole's in the Salt Tower which so encouraged John Gerard. But some are so detailed and well executed that one wonders whether a professional stone-carver was involved – a not improbable event given the casual way that prisoners were housed. In the Salt Tower there is an extraordinarily detailed zodiac, together with mathematical tables evidently used for astrological forecasts. It is actually signed 'Hew Draper of Brystow made thys spheer the 30 daye of Maye Anno 1561'. A Hugh Draper was indeed imprisoned, accused of using magic against prominent citizens of Bristol – providing incidental evidence that not all prisoners of the Tower were political.

But even Draper's zodiac is overshadowed by the extraordinarily detailed Dudley carving in the Beauchamp Tower (see picture on page 85). The five Dudley brothers (one of whom, Guildford, was the husband of Jane Grey) were imprisoned in 1553 and though all were condemned to death, along with their father, the duke of Northumberland, only Guildford went to the block. The carving shows the Bear and Ragged staff arms of the Warwicks, with the name John Dudli carved immediately beneath (he was earl of Warwick until his father's death). Surrounding the arms is a border composed of roses, gillyflowers, oakleaves and honeysuckle and underneath is a doggerel verse explaining that the plants stand for four brothers. The whole is an exercise in the visually punning device known as the rebus: the oakleaves stand for Robert (from the Latin *robur* – oak): the gillyflowers for Guildford: the roses for Ambrose and the honeysuckle for Henry.

In the Beauchamp Tower, too, is perhaps the most poignant of all the graffiti: the single name IANE carved twice – once high up on the northern wall and once lower down just below the window looking on to the Parade and site of the scaffold. The Reverend John Brand, who uncovered the inscription, believed that it was carved by Jane Grey herself, an idea denounced by the somewhat puritanical John Bayley in his massive *History*. He pointed out that the Beauchamp Tower was occupied by the Dudley brothers 'and however severe might formerly have been the treatment of state delinquents, a sense of delicacy seems always to have been preserved towards the weaker sex' and it was highly unlikely that the unfortunate girl would have been expected to share a cell with five men. Bayley's explanation, that the name was carved by Jane's husband, is probably the right one.

The IANE (Jane) inscription. The number is a nineteenth-century attempt to identify the graffiti of the Tower.

Nearly 100 of the 400-odd inscriptions that have been discovered appear in the Beauchamp Tower, probably because it was the tower most frequently used as a prison. The function of the Tower of London as a prison has been obscured by the demolitions that have taken place since the seventeenth century, in particular the wholesale destruction of the palace suite, a warren whose rooms and passages and cellars must have provided considerable accommodation. At the time of Wyatt's rebellion, for instance, at least 600 prisoners were somehow crammed into the castle in addition to the normal garrison and warders. Somewhere, certainly, was the notorious Little Ease, a prison cell so designed that it was impossible to stand, sit or lie in it. It undoubtedly existed: the first reference to it was in 1534 when a man called John Bawde was imprisoned there and it was still in use half a century later when a Catholic described his experiences in it. It is just possible that a carving in the Beauchamp Tower, showing a naked man cramped in a kneeling position in an alcove, might be an attempt to illustrate this hideous cell. By 1604, however, it had ceased to be used and its most likely locality was in the base of the Flint Tower: this was rebuilt in 1796 when all traces of the cell, if such it was, disappeared. The locality of the so-called 'dungeon of rats' is entirely unknown. This was supposed to have been a cell below the high-tide level of the Thames. As the tide rose the cell was invaded by rats seeking a refuge, creating a peculiar dimension of horror for the wretched inhabitant.

The overwhelming probability is that the Tower never possessed the specially built 'dungeons' and 'torture chambers' beloved of sensational fiction. Living conditions for most prisoners were almost certainly little worse than that prevailing for the garrison. In 1695, for instance, Christopher Wren was commissioned to survey the Beauchamp and Bloody Towers 'and report wt Expense will put them in condition to hold prisoners of State and what number they will hold'. He was extremely dubious as to their suitability: 'Both the said places were put the last summer in better repair than they have been in many years, but to make them fitt for prisoners of State (if by that Expression it be intended that they should be wainscotted and made fitt for hangings and furniture) may cost £200 or much more, but with such walls, windows and winding stairs they never can be made proper with any cost without rebuilding'. By Wren's day, the great White Tower itself was used mostly as a provision and ordnance store and his report makes clear that the mural towers were used for upper-class prisoners who would spend their own money on making them reasonably habitable. Other prisoners would be simply thrust into holes and corners on that *ad hoc* basis which seems to be a characteristic of the castle, their sufferings being incidental rather than intentional.

A frequent question put to the Yeomen Warders by visitors today is 'Where is the torture chamber?' Obligingly, the Tower authorities have laid out the ground floor of the small Bowyer Tower as a display area for 'instruments of persuasion' including a gibbet, catchpole, block and axe with two spare axe heads, 'one of several that were kept ready for use', thumbscrews, bilboes and the like. The instrument most commonly associated with the Tower, the rack, is represented only in pictorial form, for the last rack was destroyed by fire in 1841. The Tower of London, in fact, never possessed a torture chamber as such. It is the nineteenth-century novelist, Harrison Ainsworth, who in his 'historical romance' *The Tower of London* took up where Foxe left off in his *Book of Martyrs*, who bears heavy responsibility for the popular idea of the Tower as a vast prison and torture chamber. Published in 1840, at about the time that the public were becoming aware of the Tower as an historical landmark, his novel is an ingenious mixture of hard fact and lurid fiction that became immensely popular. One of his set pieces is the description of the torture chamber:

> ... a small circular chamber in the centre of which stood a heavy stone pillar. From this pillar projected a long iron bar sustaining a coil of rope terminated by a hook. On the ground lay an immense pair of pincers, a curiously shaped saw and a brasier ... Against the wall stood a broad loop of iron, opening in the middle with a hinge – a horrible instrument of torture termed the Scavenger's Daughter. Near it were a pair of iron gauntlets, which could be contracted by screws until it crushed the fingers of the wearer. On the wall also hung a small brush to sprinkle the wretched victims who fainted from excess of agony, with vinegar ...

Above Inside the Salt Tower: a fireplace (now blocked)

The 'Walpole' graffito which so comforted John Gerard

Above left The Dudley carving in the Beauchamp Tower

Above right The view from the Queen's House

Below left The Council Chamber of the Queen's House (Lieutenant's Lodgings) where Guy Fawkes and John Gerard, among many, were interrogated. Today the Queen's House is part of the Governor's Residence.

Below right The interior of the Beauchamp Tower, one of the first towers to be restored last century. The Dudley carving is to the right of the fireplace.

Opposite right The Beauchamp Tower. A major prison, this holds the largest collection of prisoners' graffiti, including the Dudley carving. To the right, behind the low railings, is the site of the scaffold for such private executions as that of Anne Boleyn.

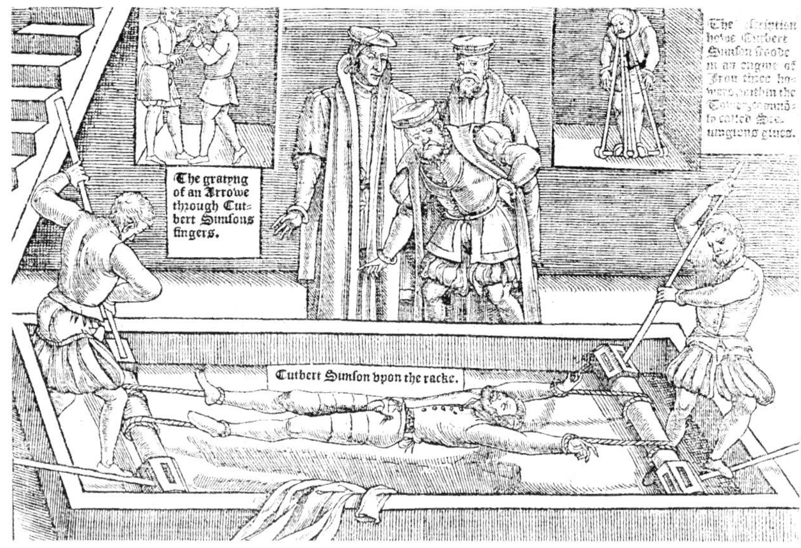

An illustration from Foxe's *Book of Martyrs*, the book very largely responsible for the Tower's sinister reputation

Torture was undoubtedly used as a matter of course in the Tower, as in all other prisons, to extract confessions. James I wrote out in his own hand, using his own eccentric orthography what confessions were to be obtained from Guy Fawkes, and how 'if he will not other wayes confesse, the gentler tortours are to be first usid unto him et sic per gradus ad ima tenditure, and so god spede youre goode worke'. Fawkes's agonized signature on his confession gives ample testimony of the efficacy of the torturers. Although the 'torture chamber' exists only in Ainsworth's imagination – the usual place for the processes was in the ground floor of the White Tower – his list of instruments is accurate enough and corresponds with those on display in the Bowyer Tower. The rack was commonly known as the Duke of Exeter's Daughter for it was introduced by the fourth duke of Exeter when he was Constable in the fifteenth century. The Scavenger's Daughter owes its name to a Lieutenant of the Tower named Skeffington who introduced the device in the reign of Henry VIII. The model currently on display in the Bowyer Tower looks deceptively simple, consisting as it does of an iron hoop and chain, but it seems to have been the most feared of all, even surpassing the rack in the agonies it inflicted. The victim's head was thrust through the iron hoop and the rods were connected by shackles to his ankles. By means of tightening screws the victim was contracted in a bent condition until he became a solid mass of agonized flesh. The pressure was so great that blood has been described as being forced through the skin.

John Gerard's apparently pedantic insistence on seeing that the warrant for his torture was correctly signed illustrates the English passion for legality that eventually brought judicial torture to an end. In 1628 an ex-soldier, John Felton, assassinated Charles I's favourite, the duke of Buckingham. The assassination was on a purely personal matter but Charles was convinced that there was a political plot against him and ordered that Felton be put to the torture in the Tower to extract the name of the supposed conspirators. Archbishop Laud presided over the interrogation and when he warned Felton that he would be put to the rack if he did not confess, Felton made the obvious reply which weakens the entire case for confession under duress: 'If I am racked, my lord, I may happen in my agony to accuse your lordship'. In those uncertain times, Laud took no chances and referred the matter back to the king who, in turn, sought to protect himself by decreeing that Felton was to be tortured 'to the furthest stretch allowed by law'. But what was that 'furthest stretch'? The bench of judges, assembled to consider the matter and anxious to protect their own backs, ruled that 'torture could not be applied according to English law' for no one was prepared to sign a warrant. Felton went to a relatively quick death at Tyburn and the instruments gathered dust until their revival as historical relics.

SECTION III THE MONUMENT

The Tower is a citadel to defend or command the city: a royal palace for assemblies or treaties: a prison of state for the most dangerous offenders: the only place of coinage for all England at this time: the armoury for warlike provision: the treasury of the ornaments and jewels of the crown: and general conserver of the most records of the king's courts of justice at Westminster.

John Stow
The Survey of London, 1598

Chapter VII
Mysteries and Murders

On 22 November 1963, John Kennedy, President of the United States of America, was murdered in full view of millions of people. The milliseconds leading up to, during and after the murder have been the subject of exhaustive investigations over many years, employing the most sophisticated techniques, drawing upon the testimonies of scores of people. Nevertheless, even now there is a massive element of doubt as to exactly who killed him, how and why. Bearing all this in mind, there is small wonder that many historical events in the Tower remain mysteries, for even if those involved did not deliberately doctor the evidence, the sheer weight of centuries, with each generation embroidering that which had gone before and the lack of documentary evidence, will ensure that a question mark will remain over many a case.

Predominant over all, of course, is the alleged murder of the princes in the Tower for it has all the elements of a folk-tale: the wicked uncle, the beautiful, innocent children, the evil murderers. The perpetrator has been identified, finally and permanently, as Richard III – and as finally and permanently as Richard's successor, Henry VII. It is even possible to assemble evidence to show that the boys were never murdered at all, but were spirited away by a third party to live out their lives in safe obscurity.

The background to the mystery is confusing enough. As prelude is the bizarre story of the murder of the duke of Clarence in a butt of malmsey wine which Shakespeare, in his re-writing of history, also laid at the door of Richard III. In 1478 George, duke of Clarence, was legally and justifiably condemned to death for plotting against his brother Edward IV and was sent to the Tower. A public execution of the king's brother was obviously undesirable but just why it was believed that this extraordinary method was chosen, it is impossible to say. One of the many explanations – and this is the most likely – is that his body was removed, after execution, in a barrel that had once contained wine.

Richard III: murderer of the princes in the Tower – or victim of Tudor propaganda?

Edward IV's own sudden death, on 9 April 1483, triggered off the most profound of all the Tower mysteries for it was his two young sons who became the 'princes in the Tower'. The elder, who became Edward V on his father's death, was not quite thirteen

Above The Lower (*left*) and Upper (*right*) Floors of the Martin Tower. This was turned virtually into a private residence for the imprisoned duke of Northumberland and was later used to house the regalia.

Left A local inhabitant: Mr Samuel Pepys, who knew the Tower of London both as prisoner and as visitor; from his bust in nearby Seething Lane

years old, while his brother Richard of York was about three years younger. In the past, succession of a minor was a certain recipe for disaster as his 'protectors' struggled for power, using him as pawn. History faithfully repeated itself, the situation exacerbated by the fact that the land was in the last convulsions of the Wars of the Roses. On one side were the Woodvilles, the unscrupulous family of the boys' mother Elizabeth Woodville. On the other side was their uncle, Edward IV's younger brother, Richard, duke of Gloucester. The most dedicated of Richard's supporters cannot deny but that he hacked his way to power with total ruthlessness, stage managing events with a skill worthy of a twentieth-century dictator. But Richard, on his side, could have argued that England desperately needed a strong centralized power, and that such power was better wielded by a legitimate member of the royal dynasty than by a parcel of provincial upstarts.

Richard showed his stage-managing skill with the meeting of the Council of Regency which, as Protector of the boy king, he called on 13 June, two months after the death of Edward IV. The meeting took place in the council chamber of the White Tower and began in a relaxed, indeed jovial atmosphere with Richard congratulating the bishop of Ely on the splendid strawberries in the garden of his palace in Holborn, and begging for some. Shortly afterwards he made an excuse to leave the meeting – presumably to make certain arrangements – and when he returned his manner had dramatically changed. Silkily he asked what punishment should be meted out to anyone who had conspired against him, Protector of the king. Lord Hastings, the Chamberlain, hesitantly said they should be treated as a traitor, while other members of the council doubtless rapidly reviewed their recent movements. Baring his withered arm, Richard screamed that he had been bewitched both by Elizabeth Woodville, and Jane Shore, the late king's mistress – and now the mistress of Lord Hastings. Whipping himself into a rage, he called for the guard. Four members of the Council were arrested while Hastings was dragged down the spiral staircase and out on to Tower Green. A baulk of timber intended for the repair of St Peter's was lying handy: Hastings's neck was forced down upon it and his head was cut off as unceremoniously as that of a chicken's, the first of the seven executions to take place within the Tower.

Thereafter matters moved rapidly. The Tower, that fortress-palace in the heart of London, was the natural power base and the Council had already secured it for the boy king. On the pretext that the child needed company, Richard induced the mother to allow the lad's brother to join him. Her agreement might well be taken as a point in Richard's favour for it is surely unlikely that she would have handed over her ten-year-old son if she seriously thought he would be in danger. The Protector followed this up with a bombshell, a stage-managed sermon by a Dr Shaw, brother of the Lord Mayor of London, saying that the two children of Elizabeth Woodville were illegitimate, for their father, Edward IV, had been married to another. It is impossible now to say whether Edward IV's sexual adventures really did mean that his marriage to Elizabeth Woodville was bigamous, but it seems to have satisfied the people of England, worn out with a long-drawn-out civil war, anxious about the future with a minor on the throne and turning to the confident, energetic duke of Gloucester. On 16 July 1483, barely three months since the death of his brother, the duke was crowned Richard III.

What happened to the princes? The last contemporary account, though an uncertain one, comes from an Italian, Dominici Mancini, who was in England at the time of Richard's coronation. After the execution of Lord Hastings, he said, the boys were moved 'into the

The princes in the Tower: another of Delaroche's romantic reconstructions

inner apartments of the Tower proper' (ie they were probably moved from the palace into the impregnable White Tower). He continued: 'Day by day they began to be seen more rarely behind the bars and windows, till at length they ceased to appear altogether. A Strasbourg doctor, the last of his attendants whose services the king enjoyed, reported that the young King sought remission of his sins by daily confession and penance, because he believed that death was facing him ... Whether, however, he has been done away with, and by what manner of death, so far I have not at all discovered'.

In July 1933 a marble urn in Henry VII's chapel in Westminster Abbey was opened and the contents reverently emptied. Those contents included a quantity of animal bones, three rusted iron nails, and human bones which, when assembled, proved to be the skeletons of two male children of around the ages of ten and fourteen. The skeletons were subjected to expert investigation, then replaced in the urn 'with a statement written on parchment recording what had been done' and the urn resealed. Later, the two anatomists who had conducted the investigation, Lawrence Tanner and William Wright, published a full report. Assuming that the murder of the princes took place *before* August 1486 (ie before the battle of Bosworth in which Henry VII overthrew Richard III and ushered in the Tudor dynasty) their ages 'correspond almost exactly with the ages of the two children whose bones rest in Westminster Abbey'. The investigators came to the conclusion that the remains of the two children were indeed the remains of King Edward V and his brother Richard, duke of York: that they had been murdered almost certainly by suffocation and that their bodies had been tumbled unceremoniously into a wooden box. Edward lay at the bottom on his back with head slightly tilted to the left: his brother Richard lay face down upon him.

The bones had been placed in the urn on direct order of King Charles II immediately after their discovery in 1674. Workmen clearing away the remains of the forebuilding which once stood on the south front of the White Tower came across a chest ten feet down beneath what had been a rubbish dump. The bones they thought at first were ordinary animal bones (doubtless some fell in while they were breaking into the chest, which explains their presence in the urn in Westminster Abbey). On discovery of the skulls someone had the sense to refer the matter to higher authority. Among them was John Gibbon, Bluemantle King of Arms, who recorded, 'I my selfe handled ye Bones Especially ye Kings Skull. ye other wch was lesser was Broken in ye Digging'. There could be no possible doubt but that the remains of two children of this age, found in this position, were those of the 'princes in the Tower' missing for 191 years. Charles II therefore ordered their reburial in the royal chapel.

But on whose orders were they murdered?

Chief witness for the prosecution of Richard III is the saintly Sir Thomas More. It is largely from More's account that the colourful story of the murder has been built up: of how the Constable, Robert Brackenbury, refused to take part in it – but handed over the keys to the villainous James Tyrell: of how Tyrell recruited one of the gaolers, Miles Forrest, to assist him and his groom John Dighton: of how Forrest and Dighton actually did the deed, suffocating the children while they slept and burying them under the Wakefield Tower. But Thomas More was only five years old at the time of the murder and, moreover, was writing under the eye of Henry VIII, son of the man who is the only other suspect in the case. And while More would not necessarily lie (and many of his details are accurate enough) he would have seen no overwhelming reason to build up a case for Richard.

The strong probability is that Richard III did indeed murder the princes – but probability is not certainty and the usurping Henry Tudor had as much reason to fear the continuing existence of the princes as did Richard. More reason, for Henry's hereditary claim to the throne of England was thin in the extreme, a fact exploited by his enemies when they arranged the impersonations by Lambert Simnel and Perking Warbeck. Simnel claimed to be the last Plantagenet, Edward, earl of Warwick, son of the duke of Clarence. Henry was easily able to destroy this claim, for the unhappy young earl had been imprisoned since his childhood, first by Richard III and then by Henry himself who removed him to the Tower after the victory at Bosworth. He was brought out, put on show to refute Simnel's claims, and then returned to the Tower. Simnel was contemptuously sent to work in the royal kitchen.

Perkin Warbeck's impersonation in 1497 had far more serious results. He claimed to be Richard, duke of York, the younger of the two princes in the Tower, who was supposed to have escaped. 'He kept such a princely countenance, and so counterfeit a majesty royal, that all in a manner did firmly believe he was extracted of the noble house and family of the dukes of York.' He was even able to raise an army of some thousands in the traditionally rebellious West Country. The rebellion failed and Warbeck was captured. Despite the fact that he had taken part in armed rebellion against the Crown, Henry VII, with quite uncharacteristic generosity, sent him to the Tower to join the earl of Warwick.

Why such leniency? 'The king's manner of shewing things by pieces and dark light hath so muffled it that it hath left it almost a mystery to this day.' So said Francis Bacon nearly a century later. What we do know is that Warbeck and the young earl of Warwick were detected in a plot to blow up the gunpowder store and so escape. Both were tried and sentenced to death, Warbeck by the noose at Tyburn and the earl by the axe at Tower Hill. Knowing Henry VII's devious nature, and the very real danger that a surviving legitimate Plantagenet represented to the usurping Tudor dynasty, it is only too likely that Warbeck was deliberately introduced into the Tower precisely to tempt the earl of Warwick into his fatal attempt to escape an imprisonment that had endured nearly all his lifetime. Warbeck, too, was better out of the way. Over three centuries later he had a supporter in John Bayley, who was more than half convinced that the imposter was indeed the duke of York: 'It is to be remembered that the contrary was never proved'.

Most victims of the Tower were enemies of – or, at least, potential dangers to – the state, but in the reign of James I the Tower's sinister machinery was used for private vengeance with the murder of Sir Thomas Overbury. Overbury's friend, Robert Carr, fell in love with Frances, countess of Essex – who happened to be married. Overbury was apalled when he learned that the Countess was seeking to have her marriage annulled in order to marry Carr, for though she was only seventeen she was, he told Carr, 'a filthy base woman, nothing but a whore' – by no means an exaggerated description of a woman who was widely believed to practise Satanism. Carr, utterly infatuated, refused to heed Overbury's warning. The countess learned of Overbury's opposition, and resolved on vengeance. Her family backed her.

Frances Howard, countess of Essex, instigator of the murder plot against Overbury

What follows is as bloodthirsty and as complicated as any of the popular tragedies of the period, beginning with a remarkably clumsy murder by poisoning and ending with wholesale executions, including that of a Lieutenant of the Tower. Robert Carr was one of King James's ambiguous 'favourites' and, through that powerful connection, he and the countess's family, the powerful Howards, succeeded in getting Overbury thrown into the Tower. Carr probably intended simply to frighten his friend into silence but the Howards wanted him out of the way: permanently. The current Lieutenant of the Tower, who happened to be 'that beast Waad', was persuaded to retire, probably with a bribe, and a Howard

Sir Thomas Overbury: an incautious opinion led to an agonizing death

nominee, Sir Gervase Helwyss, put in his place. The machinery of a Jacobean tragedy began to turn over, complete with such characters as a Mrs Turner, a brothel-keeper and acquaintance of the countess's who supplied poisons, Richard Weston, an all-purpose villain who was substituted for the warder of Overbury's cell in the Bloody Tower, and assorted accomplices through whom an extraordinary mixture of poisons were administered to the wretched Overbury.

Helwyss was in an unhappy position. Once he actually met Weston taking in Overbury's supper and carrying a phial of poison which he showed to the Lieutenant. Helwyss muttered something about 'let it be done so I know not of it'. According to later depositions, over the following weeks Overbury received arsenic in his salt, cantharides in his pepper, powdered diamonds, aqua fortis. Somewhat belatedly he began to suspect that all was not well and warned Carr that he had written a full account of the affair. Quite evidently he knew something about both the Howard family and King James himself that made his existence a danger. Efforts were redoubled to put him out of the way and he succumbed at last, horrifically, to a dose of mercuric chloride added to his enema. He was buried, on the very same day, in the chapel of St Peter, evidence of influence at the highest level.

Carr, now elevated to the earldom of Somerset, duly married his countess in a ceremony of vulgar splendour: even that not impressionable society was shocked by the dress she wore, so low cut as to display her nipples. But then the rumours began. It could scarcely be otherwise considering the number and incompetence of those involved. One by one the murderers were found guilty and executed. Weston was the first to go, followed by Mrs Turner. Her Judge, Chief Justice Coke, decreed that 'as she was the person who brought yellow starched ruffs into vogue, she should be hanged in that dress'. The hangman, in mockery, wore a ruff of yellow paper as she was despatched, cursing vilely. The Lieutenant's 'perk' of a dead man's belongings served to condemn Helwyss: 'Two days before Sir Thomas Overbury died you wished his best suit of hangings to hang in his chamber, which you knew were your fees'.

The Somersets were despatched to the Tower. The countess hysterically refused to occupy Overbury's room in the Bloody Tower, screaming that his ghost was there and she was moved into the Lieutenant's Lodgings. Both she and her husband were condemned to death. On four occasions rumours spread that they were about to be executed and vast crowds assembled on Tower Hill. But the king commuted the sentence to imprisonment. They lived, comfortably enough, in the Tower for five years but with a growing hatred for each other. Though spared the fate of their fellow conspirators theirs, perhaps, was worst of all for, released at last, they were obliged by royal command to live together, tied together in a hell of their own creation until her death at the age of thirty-seven in 1632.

There seems little doubt but that King James was involved in some unsavoury way with the Overbury murder: there seems equally little doubt but that James's grandson, Charles II, was involved in that other great mystery of the Tower, the theft of the Crown Jewels. The actual organizer of the plot, the 'front man' as it were, was the notorious 'Colonel' Blood. That percipient observer, the diarist John Evelyn, succinctly described him: 'The man had not only a daring, but a villainous, unmerciful look, a false countenance – but very well spoken and dangerous insinuating.' Blood was an Irishman, a man of violence with a liking for theatrical coups who, in a packed life, had attempted to storm Dublin Castle, capture the Lord-Lieutenant of Ireland, rescue a state prisoner while he was actually under escort, and filled in the intervals with whatever would yield excitement and cash. He was a desperado but one of considerable charm, a fact which helped him to worm his way into the royal circle. Significantly, he was on close terms with Charles II's confidant, the duke of Buckingham, who ran a species of secret service for his master.

The practice of exhibiting the Crown Jewels to the public came into being at about the time of the Restoration, perhaps one of the measures designed to generate affection for the restored monarchy. It was a good idea, but conducted on that *ad hoc*, piecemeal method which characterized so many of the Tower's activities. Charles II appointed Sir Gilbert Talbot as Master of the Jewel House – but without a salary. Talbot, in his turn, delegated the task of displaying the Jewels to a personal servant, Talbot Edwards, giving Edwards the right to charge a fee. The measure proved so popular with the public that Edwards earned a substantial unofficial salary from it: on his death, indeed, Talbot was offered 500 pieces of gold for the office.

The method of display was decidedly informal, for the regalia were kept in a cupboard in the Martin Tower. Visitors were brought into the room, the door locked and the objects then brought out of the cupboard. Blood made good use of this informality. Indulging his passion for theatricals, he posed as a clergyman, a woman accomplice passing herself off as his wife. During the display of the regalia, she pretended to be taken ill and Edwards took her upstairs to his quarters where Mrs Edwards looked after her. The pretence enabled Blood both to reconnoitre the tower and to put himself into a social relationship with the Edwardses. Over the next few days the charming Irish clergyman and his ladylike wife made several visits to the Martin Tower where they were welcomed by the septuagenarian Edwards – particularly so when it transpired that the clergyman had a wealthy young nephew who would make an excellent husband for the Edwards's daughter.

A popular representation of Blood's attempt on the Crown Jewels

Gullibility would appear to have been one of the qualifications for the role of keeper of the Jewel House. Early on the morning of 9 May the affable clergyman returned – with three male friends –

to discuss the forthcoming wedding. Casually, Blood asked if his friends could see the regalia. Edwards let them into the Jewel House when, immediately, Blood showed the violence behind the genial mask. Edwards, then in his late seventies, was seized, and a wooden plug thrust brutally into his mouth. The old man gallantly fought off his assailants: he was beaten over the head, stabbed in the stomach and thrown down. The cupboard containing the regalia was broken open.

Blood's next action was decidedly peculiar. The Martin Tower, in the north-east of the complex, lies the furthest possible distance from the entrance. After the robbery the thieves would have to run the gauntlet of the garrison and the warders across the entire length of the castle at an hour when visitors were somewhat unusual. Commonsense would have dictated that they would have taken the smallest objects in the regalia as easiest to hide in their clothing. Instead, Blood chose the massive St Edward's Crown, the Sceptre, nearly four feet long, and the heavy Orb. Chance now spoiled their well-planned project with the return, quite unexpectedly, of Edwards's son, on leave from the army. The thieves fled, dropping the Sceptre as they did so. There was a brief, fierce fight at the Byward Tower where a warder was shot and then the gang actually gained the Wharf where horses were waiting but there were overwhelmed.

What happened afterwards is wholly inexplicable unless the king had a hand in the affair. During his examination in the Tower Blood declared that he would speak to no one but the king. What transpired between the two is unknown: what is known is that Blood, far from being punished severely, received a pension. John Evelyn later met him at a dinner party where other guests were members of that close circle around the king known as the Cabal: 'How he came to be pardoned and even received to favour, not only after this, but several other exploits almost as daring, both in Ireland and here, I could never understand.' Evelyn speculated that Blood was a double agent, spying for the Crown but, while this would explain his indemnity from prosecution, it could scarcely explain the attempted theft. A possible explanation is that it was countenanced, directly or indirectly, by the king in order to replenish his chronically empty coffers. But this still does not explain why Blood chose the St Edward's Crown, which was not only bulky but the stones in it were only semi-precious. Along with the identity of the murderer of the princes, the motive for the attempted theft of the Jewels remains one of the Tower's enigmas.

Old Rowley – Charles II: was he behind Blood's attempted theft of the regalia?

Treasure figures in another of the Tower's mysteries, attested by no less a person than Samuel Pepys who spent some days in strenuous, but ultimately unsuccessful, search for it. On 19 April 1662 a certain Sir John Barkstead was hanged, drawn and quartered at Tyburn, one of the regicides who inevitably suffered at the Restoration. Barkstead had been a Lieutenant of the Tower as it had filled up with opponents of Cromwell's regime but was so hated for his cruelty and avarice that he was dismissed from office – not, however, before he had amassed a fortune in gold which he buried in the castle.

Or so Pepys was told by a 'Mr Wade of Axe Yard' six months after Barkstead's execution. On 30 October 1662 Pepys recorded the exciting news that a royal warrant had been obtained to search for the gold. It was supposed to consist of some £7,000 buried in butter firkins: when found £2,000 would go to Pepys's patron, the earl of Sandwich, with doubtless a cut to Pepys himself; £2,000 to Wade and his associates; and the rest to the king. On that same day Pepys, accompanied by Wade and a Captain Evett who was party to the 'secret' together with some workmen, went to the Tower to begin the search. In the best tradition of treasure hunts, Wade and Evett had only vague clues. After searching what would appear to be the cellars of the now dilapidated palace they decided on a cellar with an 'arched vault'. Pepys, deliberately or otherwise, gives no clearer identification of the cellar where 'after a great deal of council whether to set upon it now, or delay for better or more full advice, to digging we went until almost eight o'clock at night, but could find nothing'. They locked the cellar door and gave the key to the Deputy Governor whom Pepys describes in a scathing aside: 'Lord, to see what a young simple fantastick coxcombe is made Deputy Governor would make me mad: and how he called out for his nightgowne of silk, only to make a show to us. And yet for half an hour I did not think he was the Deputy Governor, and so spoke not to him about the business but waited for another man. But at last I broke our business to him and he promising his care we parted'.

Pepys and Wade, with Wade's mysterious 'intelligencer', resumed their digging in the Tower two days later: 'It was now most confidently directed, and so seriously and upon pretended good grounds that I myself did truly expect to speed. But we missed of all and so we went away the second time like fools'. Later Wade, Evett and Pepys met in the Dolphin Tavern where Pepys again received assurances that a mysterious 'confident' of Barkstead's had all the information. The 'confident' turned out to be a woman and it was arranged that she should come, in disguise, on their next trip to the Tower. This was done. The woman – probably Barkstead's mistress – confirmed that this was indeed the cellar where he had buried the butter firkin and the treasure hunters went to with a will, yet again pausing only for dinner 'on the head of a barrell'. They dug the cellar all over again, but found nothing. Pepys began to suspect that Barkstead 'did delude this woman in hopes to oblige her to further serving him' – a not unreasonable assumption given Barkstead's character.

Nevertheless, one more search was made, not in any cellar, this time, but in a corner of the Lieutenant's garden 'against the mayne-guard' (the wall running up from the Bloody Tower). Pepys privately thought this 'a most unlikely place' and as it was a bitter cold December day he decided to leave the work to the others: 'I did sit all the day till three o'clock by the fire in the Governor's house, I reading a play of Fletcher's being "A Wife in a Month" wherein no great wit or language.' As the short winter's day approached its end, he reluctantly left the comfort of the fireside to find that the treasure hunters had dug so deep that they had exposed the foundations of the wall. Glumly looking down into the empty hole, Pepys says, 'I bid them give over, and so all our hopes ended'.

Pepys was at that time twenty-nine years old, an ebullient, optimistic and at times somewhat socially naïve young man. But he was no fool, enjoying the confidence of his powerful patron and destined, in nine years' time, to wield power of his own as Secretary of Admiralty. The circumstantial evidence given him convinced him that 'there must be money hid somewhere by him'. Barkstead's mistress, too, seems to have been convinced enough to emerge from the shelter of obscurity to stake her claim. Had a third party removed the treasure secretly during the six months since Barkstead's execution? Or had the hated Lieutenant chosen so secure a place that the fabulous butter firkin with its thousands of gold coins still remains hidden? The Tower guards its secrets well.

CHAPTER VIII
THE TREASURE HOUSE

'Not only the records of the king and kingdom, but the evidence of every man's particular right': so parliament enunciated oratorically in the reign of Edward III during one of the endless jockeyings for position between king and commons. The reference was to the records stored in the Tower – Charter Rolls and Almain Rolls; Close Rolls, Patent Rolls, Gascoign Rolls, Welsh Rolls; Statutes, Pleas, Wills, Treaties and Truces – the corporate memory of the nation transmuted into parchment and stuffed into chests, into recesses, into obscure cupboards, into any dry corner that could be taken over by custodians hungry for space.

The English obsession with dynastic legitimacy, whereby they preferred to be ruled by foreigners without a word of English but of the blood royal rather by natives from a distant collateral: the English obsession with precedence: the English passion for conservation found expression in that almost obsessive preservation of records. In time, this would prove to be of almost literally priceless value for historians: few ancient nations can trace their history so minutely as the English. But the obsession added, too, to the problems of the Tower's custodians. Where better could the sacred records be housed than in that impregnable palace-fortress under the direct eye of whoever controlled the country whether it be absolute monarch, parliament or a constitutional monarchy?

So year by year the records grew. At first they were housed in the heart of the place, the White Tower. Then they were shifted into the Wakefield Tower where they would remain for the next three centuries, growing every year like some science-fiction monster. No attempt was made to put them in any kind of order until the reign of Queen Elizabeth when a Keeper, the scholar William Bowyer, was appointed: eight years he spent cataloguing the flood until the work was taken over by William Lambard. There is a delightful record of a conversation between Lambard and his queen when Lambard offered her his finished catalogue. She read it with vivid interest: these were no dry documents to her, but a family record. Coming to the reign of Richard II, and alluding both to his deposition and the recent rebellion of the earl of Essex she said dryly, 'I am King Richard II, know yee not that?' She asked Lambard if he had ever seen a true portrait of Richard and when he admitted that he had not, promised to send him one. At the end of the interview she congratulated him, saying, 'shee had not received since her first coming to the crowne any one thing that brought therewith so great delectation unto her'. Gloriana knew how to tie her courtiers to her, whether they be sea-dogs or librarians.

The already vast collection was threatened with destruction at the time of the commonwealth, the documents then being regarded as the instruments of a happily vanished tyranny. But paradoxically it was this same revolutionary government which took the first real steps in turning a mass of parchment into a coherent system when the Puritan propagandist, William Prynne, was made Keeper with the very substantial salary of £500 a year. The Wakefield Tower was filled to overflowing, so much so that the floor had to be supported. The disused chapel of St John in the White Tower was taken over, while the Wakefield Tower itself became a public record office where scholars now began to delve into the vast, raw mass of English history.

And still the mass went on multiplying. One receives a vivid impression of Keeper after Keeper fighting not only to preserve and to record but engaged in that endless task of the librarian and archivist: the fight for space, space, ever more space. In the early nineteenth century the White Tower was, as it were, re-captured, when the then Keeper, Samuel Lyson, established a bridgehead in it and in 1846 there were actually plans to occupy the Bloody Tower. But the Constable at that time was the formidable duke of Wellington and he put his foot down, insisting that a permanent home be found for the records outside the Tower before they entirely swamped the place. Twenty years were to pass before the Public Record Office was opened in Chancery Lane in 1867 and the records, after 800 years in the Tower, were moved there.

It was also in the nineteenth century that another centuries-old association came to an end when the Mint was moved out. Although a mint was established in London by the tenth century it was not until the thirteenth century that documentary evidence shows it established in the Tower. Officials of the Mint regarded themselves as being quite distinct from the rest for they were not Tower officials but operated under licence. The last of the provincial mints were closed in 1552 and thereafter the Tower Mint was the only authorized mint in the country. Much beautiful work was produced and the Mint came on to the tourist circuit – for which a fee was charged. Pepys visited it, 'to see the famous engraver Roettier, to get him to grave a seal for the Navy Office. And did see some of the finest pieces of work, in embossed work, that ever I did in my life . . .' Roettier was an Antwerp jeweller who had lent Charles II money during the king's exile and now reaped the reward. Perhaps his greatest claim to fame is that he designed the figure of Britannia – using as model Charles's mistress, the duchess of Richmond – which has been used ever after when a symbol for Britain is required. Isaac Newton was the Master of the Mint during the vital period when a change of currency was made necessary by the Act of Union with Scotland in 1707.

The Mint moved out of the Tower in order to expand in 1810, setting up shop just the other side of the road from the Tower. (The handsome façade still survives – though simply as a façade to a modern office block, the Mint having migrated yet again.) The Board of Ordnance expanded in its place. The tussle for space within the confines of the Tower is one of the clearest pointers to the castle's vital role in English history. The Board was the winner until its functions were transferred to the War Office in 1855.

The grotesque jousting helmet of Henry VII

Ever since its separation from the Wardrobe in the mid-fifteenth century the Office had been expanding, receiving a tremendous boost in the reign of Henry VIII – boy-like in his passion for guns and warlike equipment. Today, among the bewildering richness of the Royal Armouries which makes it perhaps the foremost museum of its kind in the world, it is the two great suits of armour of Henry's, at once gross and threatening, which attract the attention of most visitors. Appropriately, too, the Armouries hold guns from his ship, the *Mary Rose*, salvaged in the last century.

The Office, and later Board, of Ordnance discharged in effect the role of a Ministry of Defence over some three hundred years. Here the arms were actually manufactured, the Office taking over much of Tower Wharf for its gun foundries. Here they were stored, distributed as need arose on indents for campaigns within the country or into foreign parts. In addition, the Ordnance not only manufactured and supplied arms but had to create and maintain the means of distributing them in the absence of a standing army.

Horse armour of Henry VIII: the iron skirt carries the initials H and K

In consequence, the Board spread throughout the Tower, both physically and in influence. There was a tremendous expansion of arms storehouses immediately after the Restoration. The so-called New Armouries, built in 1664, are still a dominant feature, but the huge and ugly storehouse, built on the site of the old palace in 1670 and rebuilt after a fire, was demolished in 1883 when it became an affront to newly awakened antiquarian interests. It was while clearing the ground for this structure, in fact, that the bones of the supposed young princes were discovered. In 1688 a Grand Storehouse was built on the site of the present Waterloo Barracks: an indication of the prestige of the Office is shown by the fact that William and Mary were right royally entertained in the new building by the workmen themselves. This, too, was destroyed by fire in 1841. It is curious how incompetently the Tower managed its fire-fighting system, considering it had by then a resident disciplined military force. It was reported that 280,000 stands of arms were destroyed in the fire – arms of unique historical interest as well as contemporary value.

The Board had its finger in almost every Tower pie: it even appointed the astronomer John Flamsteed when, in 1675, an observatory was briefly established in the north-east turret of the White Tower. And it was the Armouries which began first to tolerate, and then to encourage, tourist visitors, although these first visitors were doubtless less interested in the antiquarian and aesthetic aspects of the displays, so much as hoping to pick up an idea or two from one of Europe's leading armament manufacturers. A German, Paul Hentzer, describes such a visit, during which he saw items which the modern visitor will also see:

> Upon entering the Tower we were obliged to quit our swords at the gate and deliver them to the guard. We were then led into the armoury where there are these peculiarities: spears out of which you may shoot: shields that will give fire four times: a great many rich halberds, commonly called partisans . . . and the body armour of Henry VIII: two pieces of cannon – the one fires three, the other seven balls at a time: two others made of wood

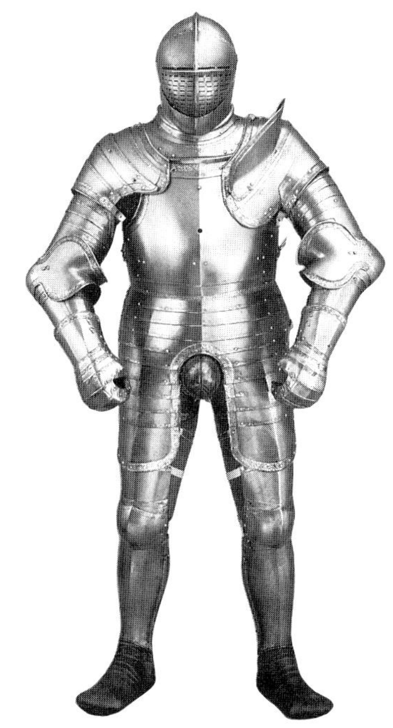

Henry VIII's armour has been a Tower attraction since the sixteenth century

EIIR

> which the English had at the siege of Boulogne: they struck a terror into the inhabitants, as at the appearance of artillery, and the town was surrendered upon articles ...

Evidently, one of the purposes of the tour was to impress foreigners, a technique carried to an impressive length by the Stuarts in their creation of the famous Line of Kings. This consisted of a series of mounted effigies of the more presentable kings of England (it is noticeable that Edward II and Richard III were absent), leading sculptors being commissioned to create the figures. In the basement of the White Tower there survives today a single horse carved by Grinling Gibbons. The display was mounted in the New Armouries and, as a kind of forerunner of Madam Tussaud's, was immensely popular. Historical accuracy was definitely secondary to propaganda: among many anachronisims was the furnishing of William the Conqueror's effigy with a musket. Similarly, the Spanish Armoury was designed to show the English how fortunate they were in their monarchs, rather than to give an accurate picture of the Armada episode. Grisly instruments of torture were on display with the information that they had been taken off ships of the Armada and had evidently been intended to subdue a beaten population. The instruments were real enough – but were actually part of the Tower's equipment, some of which are now on display in the Bowyer Tower. In 1779 Queen Elizabeth joined her line of ancestors making her famous address in Tilbury, but dressed in plate armour of a century before her time as though she were Joan of Arc.

After the decline of the Armouries as an ordnance manufactory and store, they began to develop as a museum emphasizing Britain's imperial role. In 1830 the historian John Bayley recorded that 'the armouries are deservedly the objects of general attraction to persons of all nations who visit the capital of the British empire. But,' he went on indignantly, 'the charges that are made for admission form a ground for loud and universal complaint and are justly looked upon by foreigners as a disgrace to the liberality of our national character'. The Armouries still dominate the Tower of London today: together with the small, independent Royal Fusiliers Museum, they occupy all the major buildings – the entire White Tower, the Waterloo block, the Hospital block and the New Armouries. In 1984 they were detached from the Department of the Environment to form a museum in their own right and have embarked on energetic fund-raising activities. Presumably, they will continue to turn down such opportunities as the £20 million offered by a now legendary American for Henry VIII's armour.

Second only to the Armouries in public interest was the menagerie: indeed, a guidebook of 1791 leads off with a description of the menagerie as though the Tower itself was simply an adjunct. Private zoos were prestige symbols in the Middle Ages and that of the Tower's developed out of the collection begun by Henry III when the emperor Frederick II sent him, in 1235, three leopards from his own magnificent collection in Forli. Thereafter the menagerie grew steadily, giving a name, the Lion Tower, to one of the mural towers. The plan of the Tower made by Haiward and Gascoigne in 1597 shows this to have been a semi-circular bastion just outside the Middle Tower and on the site of the present public entrance. It was fitted up elaborately with cages and trapdoors and a viewing gallery for the public.

One of the many unpleasing stories told about that unpleasing monarch James I describes how he ordered a lamb to be placed in the lion's den; the lamb, after going up and exchanging sniffs with one of the monsters, simply lay down and was eventually drawn up without harm. It was James, too, who wanted to see if an English mastiff was the equal of an African lion. In an encounter with a lion, two mastiffs were killed in succession and a third, after gallantly attacking the lion, was taken out badly injured. It was to the credit of the young Prince Henry that he ordered the surviving mastiff to be sent to St James's Palace 'and there kept and made much of, saying that he that hath fought with the king of the beasts shall never fight with any inferior creature'.

The menagerie declined badly during the Napoleonic Wars but in 1822 a new keeper, Alfred Cops, was appointed and his skill and devotion paradoxically led to the ending of the 600-year-old institution in the Tower. For, within seven years, Cops had so improved the menagerie, both in number of specimens – well over sixty – and the way in which they were housed that it began to

Opposite The Yeomen Warders frequently refer to the ravens as the only true 'beefeaters': the birds have a standard ration of beef

A nineteenth-century view of the dangers of the Tower menagerie

The menagerie in 1820, shortly before its reform

achieve both scientific as well as popular interest. So much so that the menagerie and the increasing number of its visitors began to prove a serious impediment, situated as it was at the main entrance of the Tower. The Constable now was the formidable duke of Wellington and, with that no-nonsense approach of his, he decided the menagerie must go. There was strong opposition but go it did, in 1835, the bulk of the collection being transported to the gardens of the London Zoological Society in Regents Park, forming the nucleus of the present world-famous zoo.

The connection was broken but not, perhaps, wholly ended for the six ravens now on the permanent establishment of the Tower are probably a legacy of the menagerie. How, why and when the ravens achieved their present status is quite unknown. A vague story to the effect that, if they leave the Tower, the Tower will fall and, with it, the kingdom (or, in other versions, the monarchy) is associated with Charles II – probably an unexpected spin-off from the various attempts to endear the newly restored monarchy to its still somewhat dubious subjects.

What is undoubted is that the ravens are, according to Colonel John Wynn, a Deputy Governor, 'enormously popular with our visitors, particularly with the children. Among the attractions they come behind the Crown Jewels and equal with the instruments of torture – which is pretty high'. His remark was occasioned by a lively controversy in the national press in 1987, triggered off by a letter from a French airman, Peter Kroyer, who had complained about the Tower's 'barbarous practice' in clipping the wings of what he called 'these natural aviators'. Certainly the practice, though painless, is ugly and a variety of suggestions were put forward as alternatives. One of the unfounded charges made against the Tower authorities was that the birds as fledglings 'were snatched from their mothers at an early age on a craggy Welsh mountain'. Denying the charge – traditionally, the birds have come as gifts to the Tower in their early maturity – the Tower disclosed the surprising information that there was a breeding pair

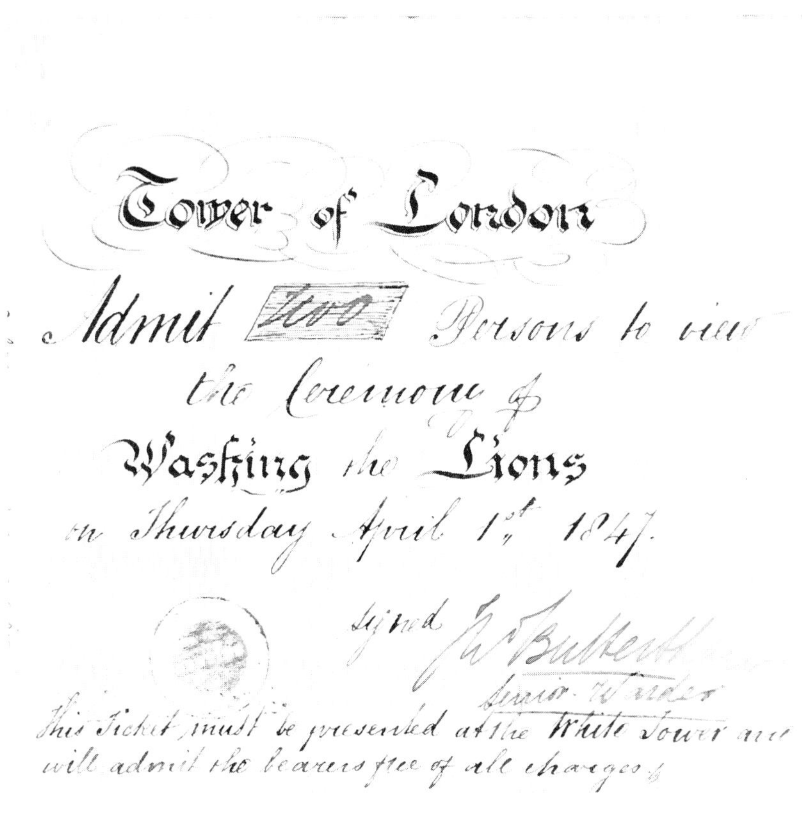
Tower of London

Admit Two Persons to view the Ceremony of Washing the Lions on Thursday April 1st 1847.

Signed [illegible] Senior Warder

This Ticket must be presented at the White Tower and will admit the bearers free of all charges.

A hoax invitation to a non-existent ceremony

on the establishment which had actually produced eggs. Hitherto it has been assumed that the birds would never mate under the artificial conditions prevailing in the Tower. The birds are in the personal charge of a Raven Master who is allocated a regular sum for their upkeep, their diet including steak and eggs. The Yeomen Warders, somewhat resentful of their universally known nickname, frequently make the remark that the Tower ravens are the only true beefeaters.

The Crown Jewels of the United Kingdom display in graphic – indeed, theatrical – form, the thesis that the splendour of a set of regalia is in inverse proportion to the actual power of the ruler who wears it. William the Conqueror, who was indubitably the ruler of England, is traditionally shown wearing a simple circlet: the present Imperial State Crown, made for Queen Victoria in 1837 and used on such state occasions as the opening of parliament, is an immense object the size of a football, weighing several pounds and smothered with jewels whose value is, quite literally, incalculable, including as it does the Black Prince's ruby and the Second Star of Africa, the second largest diamond in the world.

Visitors to the regalia tend to be surprised, and a little disappointed that there is no crown here that had been worn by Henry VIII, or Elizabeth I or Edward III – indeed, by any of the great monarchs of English history. The reason is simple: after the execution of Charles I the new republican government promptly turned these 'baubles of tyranny' into hard cash. Most of the regalia on display were made for the Restoration of Charles II, with additions for the coronations of successive monarchs.

The various accounts of the Restoration leave one with the impression of an establishment rather desperately trying to persuade itself that there had been no real break, that the English were devoted subjects of an unchanged and unchanging monarchy. Charles II's coronation procession, from the Tower to Whitehall, was probably the most magnificent of its kind; it was also destined to be the last. It took place, with deliberate intent, on St George's Day – 23 April – 1661 and Mr Pepys saw it all, hanging out of a window of 'Mr Young's the flagmaker in Cornhill. It is impossible to relate the glory of this day, expressed in the clothes of them that ride and their horses and horse-clothes . . . The king in a most rich embroidered suit, looked most noble'. London was still a relatively small town and Pepys knew many of those now riding by in unfamiliar splendour: 'Wadlow, the vintner at the Devil, did lead a fine company of soldiers, all comely young men in white doublets. There followed the Vice-Chamberlain, Sir. G. Carteret, a Company of men all like Turks, but I know not what they are for. The streets all gravelled and the houses hung with carpets before them . . . So glorious was the show with gold and silver, that we were not able to look at it, at least being so much overcome.'

The coronation had actually been postponed until the regalia had been replaced on a fitting scale at a total cost of £31,000 9s 11d. A few items had survived the holocaust, among them the twelfth-century Anointing Spoon and the eagle head of the Ampulla which held the sacred oil: a skilled craftsman made a new body for

Above The Ampulla and Anointing Spoon, the only surviving items of the pre-Caroline regalia

Left The crown worn by George V at the Delhi Durbar in 1911 and never worn since

Opposite The Imperial State Crown with the Black Prince's ruby

it. St Edward's Crown – the crown which is placed on the monarch's head at the actual moment of coronation – was also a survivor; the lower half may indeed have belonged to Edward the Confessor and was suitably refurbished. At the banquet which followed the coronation there were two splendid objects, both given by city councils who had been rather too enthusiastic in their support for the Cromwellians and now thought it advisable to make their peace with a restored monarchy: the city of Exeter gave a magnificent Salt, made in the form of a castle and Plymouth gave a Fountain. Both objects were probably made in Hamburg.

After 'Colonel' Blood's audacious attempt to steal the Jewels, security was gradually tightened. Among various measures, which included placing an armed sentry outside the door, was the provision of a sturdy metal grill behind which the objects were displayed. That grill very nearly brought about the Jewels' destruction on the night of the fire of 1841 which totally destroyed the nearby Grand Storehouse. By 11pm the heat in the Martin Tower was so intense that some of the fabrics in the showcase had begun to brown, while the onlookers could only regard the case helplessly. The only person who had the keys to the grill was the Lord Chamberlain: he was not an officer of the Tower and no one knew where he was on that terrible night. There was confusion, too, over the responsibility, for the Tower was outside the jurisdiction of the police, and the newly formed London Fire Brigade Establishment was a purely commercial organization.

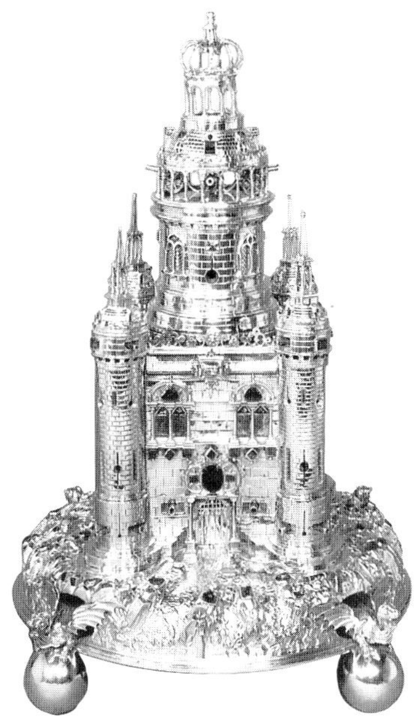

The Exeter Salt, cannily presented by the city of Exeter to mark the coronation of Charles II

A slight improvement on security for the Crown Jewels in the Martin Tower in 1840

The fire of 1841, which destroyed the Grand Storehouse and endangered the Crown Jewels

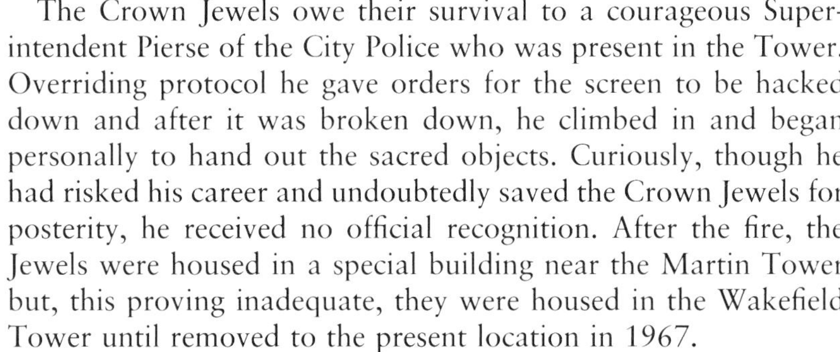

The Crown Jewels owe their survival to a courageous Superintendent Pierse of the City Police who was present in the Tower. Overriding protocol he gave orders for the screen to be hacked down and after it was broken down, he climbed in and began personally to hand out the sacred objects. Curiously, though he had risked his career and undoubtedly saved the Crown Jewels for posterity, he received no official recognition. After the fire, the Jewels were housed in a special building near the Martin Tower but, this proving inadequate, they were housed in the Wakefield Tower until removed to the present location in 1967.

The modern Jewel House is a triumph of architecture and display. Situated in the west wing of the Waterloo block, it is on two floors. The ground floor of the Waterloo block is devoted largely to civic plate and maces. The regalia proper are housed in a strong room far below ground to which access is gained by a curving staircase down through untreated concrete walls and then through a massive door. The lighting in the Jewel Chamber itself is kept to a deliberately low level so that the regalia, in their elegant bullet-proof glass case, blaze out like one vast jewel. There are two walkways around the case, the lower permitting the visitor to approach the glass and so come within inches of the objects within. Those using this walkway, however, are kept in continual movement: for prolonged inspection it is necessary to ascend to the upper walkway some two or three yards distant from the showcase.

The inescapable question which the custodians answer with varying degrees of patience is, 'What are they worth?' To which the inescapable answer is, 'Impossible to say. They're priceless'. The object which, if broken up, would fetch the highest price in a jeweller's is probably the Imperial Crown of India: this, too, illustrates the thesis that a set of regalia approaches its apogee as a showpiece as it begins to approach its political nadir. In the past, the monarchs of England have tended to regard their regalia as negotiable currency – a fact not unknown to Charles II. In order to prevent disposal abroad, the constitutional practice has been to prevent any of the crowns of England from leaving the country. When, therefore, the great 1911 Durbar of Delhi was planned, the Maharajahs of India sent a quantity of precious stones to England to be made into the Imperial Crown. The coronation in Delhi took place as the first rumblings of discontent in the Indian subcontinent heralded the dissolution of the empire upon which the sun never set. The Crown has never been used since.

Chapter IX
The City within a City

> All the Tower's history is past, and the chance of a memorable place to look at was lost with the preposterous mock-medieval outer walls of the 1840s, probably by Salvin, every bit as silly as Windsor and far less fun. The atmosphere makes even the real events seem phoney. People actually went to their deaths through that pasteboard Traitors' Gate? Nonsense.

So said the late Ian Nairn in his lively survey of London's monuments, published in 1966. Britain owes a lot to Nairn, not least for his identifying of, and savage attack on, the creeping suburbanization of the country to which he gave the memorable name of 'Subtopia'. But he is being less than fair to Anthony Salvin. Britain was in the grip of the 'Gothic revival'. All over the country the past was being interpreted in terms of gargoyles and turrets, crockets, pointed arches, stained glass. Had Salvin followed that fashion, then we would have ended up with a Walt Disney creation like the Law Courts in the Strand, built at about the same time. Salvin could be as exuberant as any of his fellow architects, as witness his restoration of Alnwick Castle in Northumberland among many. But in the thirty-odd years he worked on the Tower of London he restrained himself as far as design was concerned. His Waterloo block is immediately recognizable as 'Victorian Gothic' but it was a completely new building raised on the site of the fire-destroyed Grand Storehouse. Purists might regret his refacing of the Beauchamp Tower and the almost complete rebuilding of St Thomas's Tower (Traitors' Gate) but both were made necessary by the physical conditions of the buildings. He was, in any case, following a long established tradition of successive generations adapting the great castle for current needs – the Tudor range containing the Lieutenant's Lodgings is startlingly different from the White Tower, from which it is separated by over 400 years. Apart from the obvious Victorian buildings in the north and north-east part of the Tower of London, it is safe to say that very few among the Tower's millions of visitors are aware of the substantial Victorian restorations.

The final transformation of the Tower took place under the eagle eye of Arthur Wellesley, duke of Wellington, appointed Constable in 1826 and turning that largely honorary office into an effective instrument of change. Apart from checking the proliferation of records and easing out the menagerie, he arranged for the draining of the moat, turning a malodorous source of illnesses into an attractive green sward. It was under Wellington's administration, too, that the very last military changes were made to the Tower when, under the threat of Chartist riots in the 1840s, he had a bastion constructed on the north wall of the Tower in order to dominate the natural assembly point on Tower Hill. In the event it was never used and was subsequently demolished. But the fact that the Tower still had a potential military role was shown by the anxiety over the construction, in 1893, of Tower Bridge. For the first time in its history the Tower was dominated by a neighbouring structure, and a paragraph was inserted into the Tower Bridge Act giving the garrison right of access to the Bridge when necessary.

As with all long-established British institutions, the administration of the Tower of London is almost unbelievably complicated as, over the centuries, new functions have been grafted on to old, and obsolescent functions continued on a ceremonial basis. Rights and duties are spread over a wide range of officials, from hard-headed anonymous civil servants to glamorous, but purely decorative,

Above The Chief Yeoman Warder in front of his lodgings

Left above The Quay. It is from here that ceremonial gun salutes are fired.

Below The Casemates (chambers in the thickness of the curtain wall) form lodgings for the Yeomen Warders

Opposite Nineteenth-century restorations and additions at the Tower

figureheads. While researching the present book the author, working through a sheaf of telephone numbers, was startled to find himself talking to someone in Buckingham Palace. An example of the Tower's literally extraordinary situation is that its chapels – including that of St Peter ad Vincula – are classed as 'chapels royal', that is, chapels totally outside the bishops' jurisdiction and responsible only to the monarch. Within the Tower, the Armouries and the Fusiliers Museum are totally separate from the administration (the visitor actually has to pay a small entrance fee to enter the Fusiliers Museum). In some not very clearly defined manner, the artefacts are cared for by English Heritage, the quasi-independent, but official body which administers Stonehenge among other ancient monuments. But English Heritage has no powers to regulate tourism within the Tower. This regulation of tourism is a vital role, bearing in mind the fact that in 1986–7 the Tower generated an income of £6.7 million which in most years allows it to break even. Tourism is administered by the same sub-division of the Department of the Environment which administers the royal palaces of Hampton Court, Kensington and the Banqueting Hall in Whitehall. But the Department shares those powers with the Officers of the Tower.

Another source of confusion is that the role and titles of the senior Officers have changed again and again over the centuries. The supreme office of Constable was, quite early on, regarded as a purely ceremonial role unless, like the duke of Wellington, the Constable deliberately exerted his powers. Duties were delegated to a Lieutenant – but from the early eighteenth century onwards the Lieutenant also ceased to live in the Tower, delegating his duties to a Deputy Lieutenant, responsible for prisoners, and a Major who was increasingly responsible for the military side. During Wellington's administration, the office of Major emerged as the more important of the two and in 1858 was referred to as the 'Resident Governor'. This is the title born by the chief officer in residence today, his two Deputies being known not as Deputy Lieutenants but as Deputy Governors.

In 1727, during Williamson's regime, the commander of the Tower garrison flatly disobeyed an order from him, bringing to a head a longstanding dispute as to who, ultimately, controlled the Tower. Williamson complained to the Constable, Lord Lonsdale, who in turn complained to the king. George II responded with a thunderbolt: 'OUR WILL AND PLEASURE IS THAT, the Constable, Lieutenant, Deputy Lieutenant or other Officer of the Tower have the Command and Direction of everything relating to the Tower'. Since the late eighteenth century, the office of Constable has always been filled by a distinguished soldier, usually a Field Marshal, eliminating that possible source of friction. Until 1938, the appointment of a Constable was for life, but since then it has been for a term of five years, the Constable holding his office by Royal Letters Patent under the Great Seal, and with the privilege of direct communication with the monarch. The first Constable of the post-war years was the hero of the Western Desert and late Viceroy of India, Field Marshal Earl Wavell.

'On the 22nd Day of August 1475 Henry, Earl of Richmond was by public Acclamation saluted on the Battle Field of Bosworth King over England and was crowned [Henry VII] on the 30th Day of October following. In the first year of his reign, the Yeomen of the Guard was first ordered o'er which the Yeomen Waiters or Warders of the Tower hath the seniority.' In time, the Yeomen Warders of the Tower became distinct from the Yeomen of the Guard, who provide a personal escort for the monarch on state occasions, and the fact that they are invariably confused lies largely at the door of Gilbert and Sullivan. Gilbert wanted, correctly, to call their opera *The Beefeaters* – 'a good sturdy, solid name' said he – but the more genteel Sullivan thought it ugly and their opera was launched into history with its misleading title.

Gilbert might have been correct, but his wish to use the nickname is not one which would endear him to the present Warders: 'To call us Beefeaters is like calling an American a Yank, a German a Kraut or an Englishman a Limey. It's not exactly insulting – but it's not very polite'. And it is noticeable that the Warders will, with some care, refer to themselves and each other as 'Yeoman Warder'. A well-meaning, would-be philologist dreamed up a nonexistent French word '*buffetier*', arguing that 'beefeater' was derived from the name of one serving from a buffet for the king's banquet. The magisterial *Oxford English Dictionary* gives the true, literal meaning when it defines 'beefeater' simply as 'one who eats beef' and then adds meaningly 'a well-fed menial'. One can understand why Londoners, scrabbling for a precarious living and envying the Warders their secure and well-paid posts, came up with such a mocking name, even as one can understand the modern Warder rather resenting the name, but resigned to it.

At the time of the Gunpowder Plot Sir William Waad, Lieutenant of the Tower, recorded his profound dissatisfaction at the way in which the Warders were recruited and how they discharged their duties:

> Anciently the Warders held their places only by a Bill of His Majesty and since His Majesty's coming to the crown, these

> grants are passed under Great Seal whereby great inconvenience doth arise for they have no care, many of them, to execute their office but perform their [work] by deputy and seldom come to give attendance ... some bankrupts, some given to drunkeness and disorder ... Another inconvenience cometh thereby, also by selling their places to unfit persons so that he that hath a place for his own life, doth sell the same to another for that person's life.

There was little Waad could do about it for the source of the grants came from the corrupt men around the king himself and matters continued in that vein.

In the nineteenth century that great disciplinarian, the duke of Wellington, cast a cold eye upon the chaotic situation. A particular abuse was the system whereby the Yeoman Warder bought his position – 250 guineas (£309) in Wellington's day – and made a profit by selling the facilities which he controlled. On retirement, or when he had decided he had made enough, he could re-sell his appointment to the next comer. Other important posts were in the gift of various officers, or even people who had no connection with the Tower whatsoever. Wellington abolished the system, substituting his own, and his reforms form the basis of recruitment today.

The Tower officers and Yeomen Warders share the same background – the Armed Services: Army, Royal Marines and, today, the Royal Air Force. Recruitment can be by word of mouth or by ordinary advertisement but the basic qualification is that the recruit must have spent at least twenty-two years in the Services, must be a warrant officer and have been discharged with the Long Service and Good Conduct Medals. The new Warder goes through an impressive ceremony on the Tower Green when, accompanied by his future comrades, he is formally asked by the Governor if he wishes to become a Warder. On assenting, he takes an elaborate oath and afterwards at the Yeomen Warders' Club he is welcomed with the time-honoured toast, 'May you never die a Yeoman Warder', a reference to the period when a retiring Warder could sell his post and so gain a refund of his own initial purchase. The modern Warder is on a salary, working shifts on six days a week, retiring at the age of sixty (though this can be – and quite evidently is – frequently extended). Total population of the Tower is around 150 people, with currently between forty-five and fifty families. Each family pays a rent of about ten per cent of salary, as well as such ordinary costs as electricity, water and gas charges. Rates, too, are levied, the Tower coming within the rating district of the London borough of Tower Hamlets.

Most of the lodgings, as they are called, are in the Casemates, the chambers within the thickness of the encircling wall, approached by lanes from which the public is strictly excluded. The standard of comfort is high, though most lodgings are rather dark as all windows naturally look inward into the narrow lane. Other quarters are in the Waterloo block and the Hospital block. The Resident Governor lives in the Lieutenant's Lodgings (now known as the Queen's House) while one of the Deputies lives in St Thomas's Tower.

'It's a bit like living in a goldfish bowl', one of the wives confessed. 'At times you feel that you want to scream if you see another face. And it's difficult for the children. At first they rather like saying to their friends "We live in the Tower" and watching their faces. But later on, when they realize they just can't bring their friends in as they want and they themselves have to have a pass and book out if they're going to be later than 10pm, the gilt rather wears off the gingerbread.' At night, and at weekends, the Tower is isolated, with the City dead around it, so that the community becomes necessarily inward turning. Even the humdrum business of domestic shopping becomes a problem, for the nearest ordinary shopping locality is in Whitechapel some considerable distance away. Nevertheless, with all the constraints and pressures, the Tower community seems to live a remarkably normal life and few of the Warders voluntarily relinquish their positions after the one-year probationary period.

The role of the Yeomen Warders is essentially that of public relations and guiding. All the mural towers open to the public will have a Warder on duty, changing over at regular intervals. One of the obligations of a new Warder is to study the history of the great castle in depth. He then takes the Governor and Chief Warder on a personally guided tour and only when the Governor is satisfied that the Warder is *au fait* with the history does the Warder come into contact with the public. Regularly throughout the day, the

Opposite The Changing of the Guard on Tower Green

Above The medieval standard of accommodation in the castle was at least as high as that prevailing in the outside world, as shown by this representation of a knight's chamber in the Broad Arrow Tower

public can take part in a guided tour. This usually starts near the Traitors' Gate, goes on to the steps near the Coldharbour entrance of what used to be the palace, on to the great set-piece, the site of the scaffold where bloodcurdling tales are told with relish, and culminates in St Peter's, the only circumstances in which the public is allowed to enter the chapel. No fee is charged though the Warders continue the time-honoured custom of accepting tips.

The Yeomen Warders of the Tower of London are undoubtedly the most photographed public officials in Great Britain. Their spectacular Tudor livery, however, is largely a Victorian confection. Whatever was the livery granted by Protector Somerset in the sixteenth century, it had clearly gone out of use by the eighteenth century when the Deputy Lieutenant was obliged to reprove his Warders for their appearance and urge them to make waistcoats to appear in when on duty. The present livery owes its existence to that nineteenth century wave of antiquarian interest which, among other anachronisms, created the Scottish 'tartans'. The splendid scarlet and gold livery, introduced in 1858, is worn only on state occasions: the normal livery of the Warders is the more practical blue 'undress' introduced in 1885.

The duke of Wellington actually wanted to exclude the public from the Tower in order to enhance its military security. Ever since his time, however, the Tower authorities have been gradually developing its potential as a tourist attraction. More and more of the mural towers are being opened to the public – currently, there is a plan to re-create the ingenious lifting device in the Cradle Tower. The wall walk has been steadily extended so that it is now possible to walk around about half the encircling walls, receiving dramatic views of both inside and outside the complex. The Tower, too, has benefited from the modern revolution in museum display which, while maintaining rigorous academic standards of accuracy, nevertheless tries to show artefacts in an imaginative context instead of in inert displays. In addition to laying out the upper chamber of the Wakefield Tower as Henry III's throne room, a chamber of the Broad Arrow Tower has been furnished as it would have appeared when occupied by a knight in 1381. Some of the artefacts are historic survivals; some, like the bed and chest, modern reproductions from authentic designs. Looking at the coarse but clean bed linen on the attractively chunky bed, and the great fireplace with its elegant hood, it occurs to the visitor that life within the Tower of London must have compared very favourably with the life of the citizens immediately outside its great walls.

Epilogue
The Tower and the Hill

Midsummer's Day, Tuesday 21 June 1988. Although it is a brilliant summer's morning, the lighting in this great, pillared eighteenth-century hall of the Mansion House of the Lord Mayor of London is entirely artificial, coming from gleaming chandeliers. The company that has gathered is also somewhat incongruous for the ladies are dressed as for a garden-party in light, brightly coloured clothes and picture-hats while the gentlemen are soberly dressed as befits City folk – although some of them are wearing multi-coloured and befurred robes for they are here on ceremonial duty as Aldermen and Beadles of City wards.

Separating the crowd into two equal portions and so providing an avenue leading to two throne-like chairs are two lines of men dressed in brilliant scarlet, wearing scarlet peaked caps and holding great oars upright to form a ceremonial avenue. These are holders of Doggett's Coat and Badge, élite members of the Company of Watermen and Lightermen who have sponsored the coming ceremony. There is a stir of anticipation, then two figures walk side by side down the avenue – the Lord Mayor of London and his Lady Mayoress. They approach the chairs, turn and remain standing. A moment later, and a deputation moves down the avenue towards them, its leader bearing a velvet cushion upon which lies a single red rose; the leader begins his speech.

'I am honoured to have been invited by the Master of the Company of Watermen and Lightermen to be the Chief Escort to the Knollys Rose, the red rose that the illustrious Sir William Walworth, a Fishmonger Lord Mayor in 1381, commanded Sir Robert Knollys and Constance, his wife, to pay every year to the Lord Mayor as a fine for the "haut pas" or footbridge that Lady Knollys had built across Seething Lane without consent whilst her husband was away at the wars in France ... Earlier this morning, accompanied by the Master of the Watermen's Company and his Lady and the Clerk, together with the Vicar of All Hallows by the Tower, I went to the rose garden in Seething Lane and plucked this red rose which is now my privilege and humble duty to present to you, my Lord Mayor, in payment of the penalty imposed 607 years ago.'

The Lord Mayor accepts the Rose with grave courtesy, then welcomes the assembled company as guests 'to my home'. 'My home' is an eighteenth-century building which, though immense, is almost lost among the grandiloquent Victorian and Edwardian monsters that are its neighbours in the heart of the City. It is situated on the very edge of what was that little Walbrook stream which separated the ceremonial buildings of Roman London from the rest, and along whose banks were built the private palaces of the Roman city. Listening to the Lord Mayor returning the speech, one becomes, suddenly, vividly aware of the fact that two monarchs have their seat in London, one hereditary and for life, the other elected and for a year and one would be hard put to know which court wields the greater influence. Their jurisdiction meets precisely on Tower Hill.

Ascension Day, Tuesday 12 May 1987. At 3pm a procession emerges from All Hallows by the Tower and begins to move down the Hill. It is led by a Cross-bearer at the centre of a group of grey-clad men and women. Following are clergy in black and white, a group of exuberant schoolboys carrying long wands and a mixture of layfolk and City magnates in their appropriate robes as Beadle or Alderman. As they move downhill and away from the church they are joined by ordinary members of the public, including tourists.

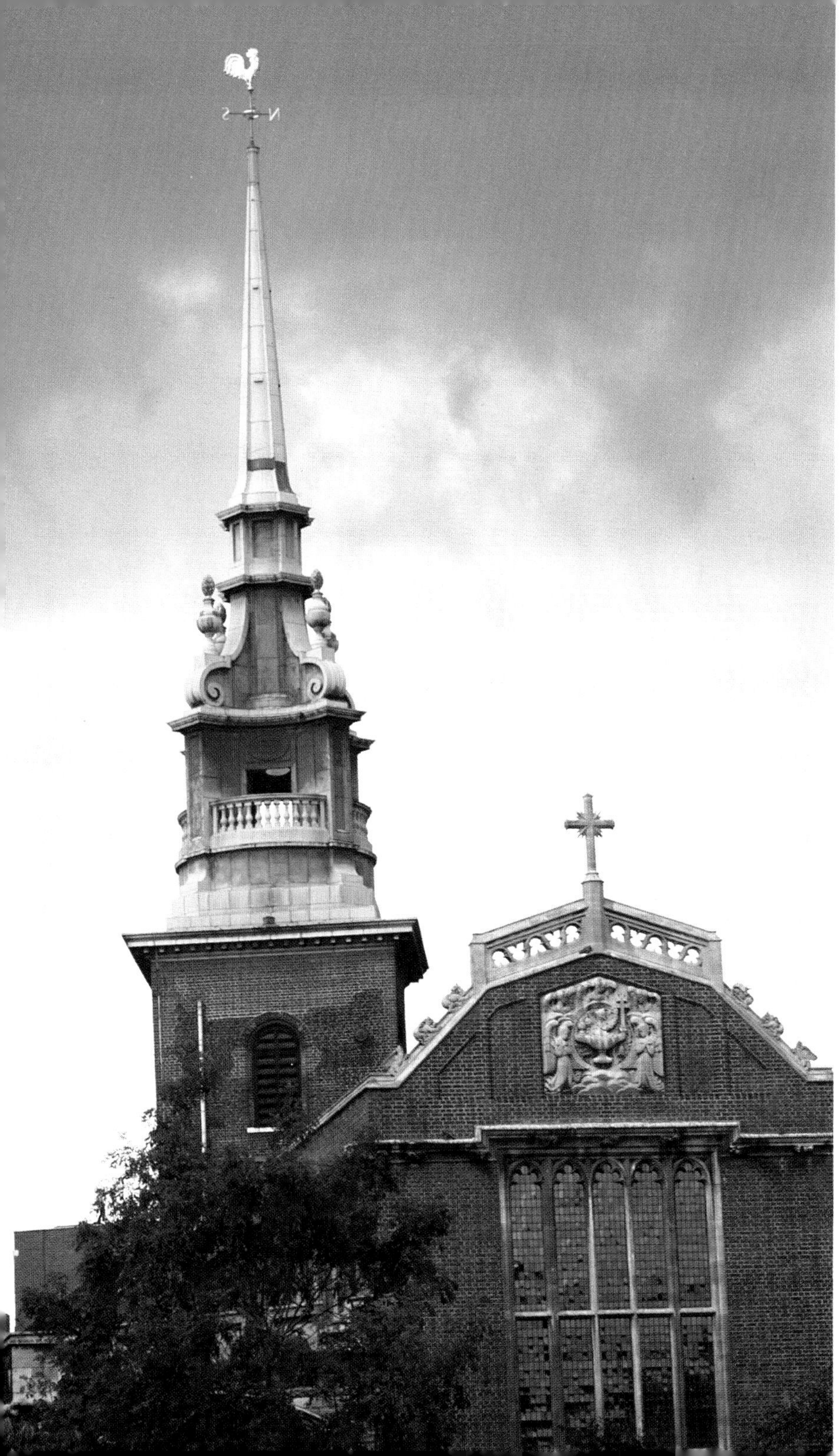

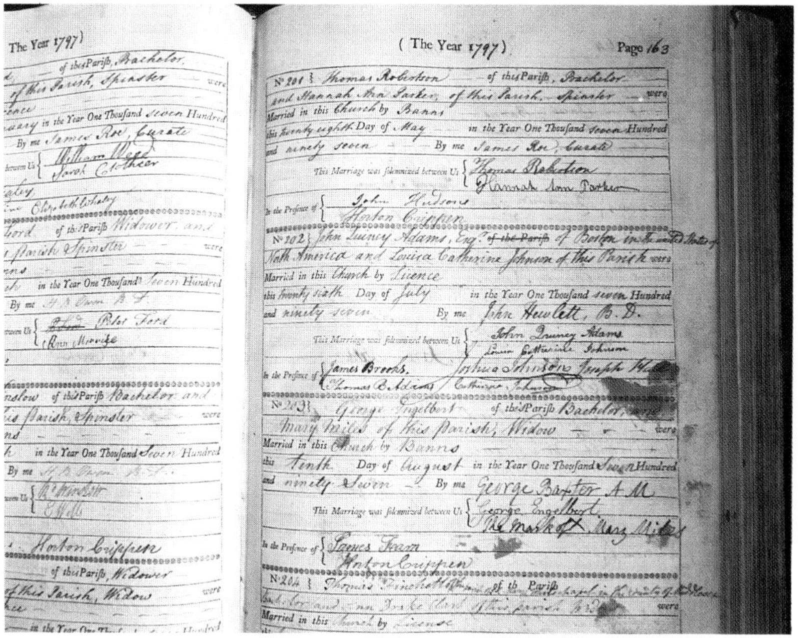

The Year 1797

(The Year 1797) Page 163

No 201 Thomas Robertson of this Parish, Bachelor
and Hannah Ann Parker, of this Parish, Spinster were
Married in this Church by Banns
this twenty eighth Day of May in the Year One Thousand seven Hundred
and ninety seven By me James Roe, Curate
This Marriage was solemnized between Us { Thomas Robertson / Hannah Ann Parker
In the Presence of { John Hudson / Hinton Crippen

No 202 John Quincy Adams, Esq. of Boston in the United States of
North America and Louisa Catherine Johnson of this Parish were
Married in this Church by Licence
this twenty sixth Day of July in the Year One Thousand seven Hundred
and ninety seven By me John Hewlett, B.D.
This Marriage was solemnized between Us { John Quincy Adams / Louisa Catherine Johnson
In the Presence of { James Brooks / Thomas B. Adams / Joshua Johnson / Joseph Hall / Catherine Johnson

No 203 George Engelbert of this Parish Bachelor and
Mary Miles of this parish, Widow were
Married in this Church by Banns
this tenth Day of August in the Year One Thousand Seven Hundred
and ninety seven By me George Baxter A.M.
This Marriage was solemnized between Us { George Engelbert / The mark of X Mary Miles
In the Presence of { James Fearn / Hinton Crippen

No 204 ...
Married in this Church by License

Above The Armada Cross, another of All Hallows's maritime relics, taken from a galleon of the Spanish Armada

Opposite left All Hallows Church on Tower Hill: the church's tower miraculously survived both the Great Fire of 1666 and the bombardments of the Second World War

Opposite right above The nave of All Hallows. Suspended ship models show the church's ancient links with the port.

Opposite below All Hallows register, showing the entry for the marriage of John Quincy Adams, sixth president of the United States

Above The axe and the block *Below* The site of the scaffold on Tower Hill

Beating the Bounds: the Tower party exiting

At about the same as this procession is emerging from the church, another is emerging from the Tower. This is led by the Chief Warder, resplendent in full ceremonial dress and bearing on his shoulder the Mace of the Tower – a silver model of the Tower itself on a long staff. Behind him comes the Chaplain followed by a group of schoolboys also bearing long wands, then an assortment of layfolk of both sexes, mostly residents of the Tower, and finally a detachment of Warders. The two groups meet about halfway down the Hill for the ritual confrontation. The schoolboys throw themselves into it with enthusiasm, capering, making disrespectful gestures to their opposite numbers – gestures echoed even by the adults. Later one of the staider members of the church party remarks, 'Perhaps we went a bit too far this year', but no lasting damage is done and there is an undertone of pride to his remark.

All Hallows Church beats its bounds every year, whereas the Tower observes the custom only once every three years, so the Confrontation is only a triennial event. It is a lighthearted re-enactment of what was once a very real, and very grim, struggle between Tower and City. In 1698 the Churchward's report records that, during the beating of the bounds that year, 'Several Warders of the Tower violently set upon him [the Churchward] and those who accompanied him in perambulation only for standing on the steps at the lower end of Tower Street, leading to the Hill – within the known, ancient bounds of the parish – to prevent them making their accustomed procession on Tower Hill'. The Warders vigorously used their halberds and several parishioners were badly injured.

The friction arose from the Tower's almost neurotic dislike of being overlooked: even today, the owners of the immense Bowring office block, built within the forbidden range of a bow-shot in the 1960s and looming over All Hallows Church, have taken out an insurance policy in case the Tower raises an objection. The Tower Liberties, a wide area surrounding the Tower over which the Crown claimed jurisdiction, was established at least from the fourteenth century: the invaluable plan by Haiward and Gascoyne clearly shows their extent in 1597. Any encroachment by the City was sternly resisted, even though the intention was benign. In 1595, when there was rioting between Apprentices and Warders on Tower Hill, the Lord Mayor turned up with the best of intentions to put an end to the trouble – but was rebuked by the Tower authorities because he was carrying the City's great Sword of State within the Liberties. The Liberties ceased to exist in 1894 when they were with the County of London but the formation of Metropolitan and City police forces contributed to the confusion. In 1933 the reverend 'Tubby' Clayton, the vicar of All Hallows who almost single-handedly brought self-respect back to Tower Hill, was profoundly shocked to find that there was 'an ugly No Man's Land between the boundaries of the City and the Metropolitan Police'. And during research for this book, a telephone call to the Metropolitan Police asking if they had jurisdiction in the Tower produced a debate rather than an answer. A slightly puzzled voice replied, 'I suppose if someone were pinching the Crown Jewels we could go in' but was interrupted by another voice saying, 'No, we can't. We'd have to get permission'. It transpired, in fact, that the Yeomen Warders are sworn in as Special Constables.

The maritime nature of the locality placed its imprint on Tower Hill. For centuries, Tower Wharf discharged the function that Victoria Station was to discharge in the railway age, and Heathrow in the age of air transport – the place where foreign dignitaries arrived and were greeted. The greeting was sometimes conducted with more enthusiasm than discretion, as Adam Williamson, the Deputy Lieutenant, recorded. On the arrival of the Hollands (Dutch) Ambassador he ordered that the saluting guns should not be fired until the coaches had left the wharf, 'it having happened on an embassy that the horses of a coach took fright by firing too soon and they and the coach fell off the wharf into the river'. Earlier, Pepys recorded how the entourages of the French and Spanish ambassadors fell to blows over precedence during a reception: the Spaniards won, with deaths on both sides.

Pepys lived in a house on Seething Lane to be near his work in the Navy Office, not far from the Tower, bringing his lively observation to bear on Tower Hill. Now he is 'dogging' a pretty lady to her home on the Hill, now escaping a creditor by bolting down one of the narrow streets, now watching executions, among them the regicides. He even got a closer view of the Tower than he could have wished for when he was briefly imprisoned in 1679 on a charge of maladministration. But the king sent him a fat buck for his dinner and insouciantly he entertained his fellow diarist John Evelyn to a meal and was out again as lively as ever. It was he who first noted a characteristic of Tower Hill which was to continue into our time, its role as a stage for labour unrest, particularly among seamen: 'Upon Tower Hill saw about 3 or 400 seamen get together: and saw one standing upon a pile of bricks, with his handkerchief upon his stick, and called all the rest to him, and several shouts they gave. This made me afeard so I got home as fast as I could'. In the late nineteenth and early twentieth century this was the natural place for the dockers to assemble to express their grievances. Clayton remarks that 'The Hill gains something of solemn dignity in that here, and here alone, the organized workers can be summoned centrally. It takes no more than four and twenty hours to fill the Hill from end to end with men determined to win what they believe to be justice. If they are ill-led bloodshed will follow. This, then, is the nature of "the Hill"'.

Unemployed gathering in 1930. The building behind is the 'monstrous warehouse' destroyed in 1940.

Above Tower Hill from the tower of All Hallows Church. The aerial bombardment of the Second World War has again made this a vast open space (compare with the 1597 plan on page 2). The Tower of London and the river lie to the right. Beneath the arch of the rainbow is the Roman city wall (detailed on page 17). The site of the scaffold (detailed on page 117), where hundreds perished, is in the left middle ground.

Opposite Night

At the very heart of Tower Hill, providing its dynamism, is the beautiful little church of All Hallows. Founded some 400 years before the Tower it was at once rival and ally of its great neighbour. When the dispute as to who had the right of execution was settled in favour of the City, it was a priest from All Hallows who would attend the victims on the scaffold during their last moments on earth; usually, too, those victims would be buried in the crypt or the yard of the church. Under 'Burialls Ano Do 1644' the Register records 'William Laude Archbishop of Canterbury. Beheaded'. But elsewhere the Register records the baptism of William Penn, founder of Pennsylvania, and the marriage of John Quincy Adams, later sixth president of the United States. Rebuilt in the sixteenth century, the church survived the Great Fire (Pepys watched the holocaust from the church's tower) but succumbed to the air raids of December 1940, the tower alone surviving. It was completely rebuilt after the War.

Physically, All Hallows encapsulates the history of Tower Hill, from the Roman pavement and Saxon crosses in the crypt to the exquisite models of ships that hang in the nave, votive offerings that emphasize the locality's connection with the sea. One of the church's treasures, indeed, is the Armada Cross, an ivory crucifix from one of the great Spanish galleons, that was perhaps given as a thank offering. But despite the church's long and rich history, perhaps its most famous vicar – and certainly the one to whom Tower Hill today owes the most – is the Reverend P T B Clayton. As an army chaplain in the First World War he founded, in the Hell of the Western Front, the haven known as Toc H where young men, their nerves shattered almost beyond repair, found a modicum of peace. Appointed to All Hallows in 1922 and working in conjunction with Lord Wakefield, who founded the still-functioning Wakefield Trust, Clayton threw himself into the task of regenerating Tower Hill, not hesitating to cross swords with the all-powerful Tower authorities. In his semi-autobiographical book *The Pageant of Tower Hill* he tells of his astonishment, on arriving at Tower Hill, 'to find that an old feud between the Tower and All Hallows had lingered on for centuries: this then was my

The moat turned into allotments under the need to produce more food in the Second World War

inheritance'. He set about healing the breach, and in due course was on amiable terms with the Governor. 'Next came the need of finding an official occasion on which I might myself be asked within the Tower. The Lieutenant Governor consulted, as was due, a Tower official. "I am thinking of asking Mr Clayton to preach at our Harvest Festival. Have you heard of Mr Clayton?" The grim reply was this. "Yes, Sir, I have heard of Mr Clayton and from what I have heard I should not think he would be at all suitable." In spite of this discernment, the invitation came.'

Two remarkable concessions were wrung from the Tower: permission for the public to use the moat for recreational purposes and the setting aside of the beach in front of Tower Wharf as the Children's Beach. The Second World War ended both concessions, but the Beach was opened again to children after the War. The ladder down to it had been destroyed by a flying bomb, but a wooden companionway that had been removed from the heroic P & O liner *Rawalpindi* when she was converted into an armed merchant cruiser was substituted. The Beach was in use in the 1950s but the custom subsequently died away, presumably falling off with the dwindling numbers of residents in the area.

Clayton had a strong social conscience, ceaselessly campaigning for the unemployed who flocked into his parish, 'the Eastern Gate of the City of London' as he called it. But he also had a strong taste for pageantry and colour – it was he who revived both the ceremony of the Beating of the Bounds and of the Knollys Rose. Under him and his successor, Peter Delaney, All Hallows has again become a focal point. The vast, otherwise anonymous commercial organizations in the area have become associated in its work: its churchwardens might live many miles away in the depth of the country but they throw themselves enthusiastically into the brilliant services that draw congregations out of what seems the unpromising surrounding commercial desert.

But it was the physical aspect of Tower Hill which particularly engaged Clayton's attention. Even in the years between the wars when the adjoining docks were operating at full capacity, this was an increasingly depressing area. A particular horror was a vast warehouse which, in 1864, had been dumped down almost in the churchyard, blocking out all view of the church from the east as well as imprisoning it behind a brutal brick barrier. The warehouse's speculative builder, Myers, in recompense gave a 'stained glass' window to the church – whose colours ran in the first rainstorm. In his book Clayton notes, 'In 1948 the lease runs out. What then?' In the event the *Luftwaffe* solved that particular problem, the monster going up in the same firestorm which destroyed the church.

Tower Hill presents a remarkable example of an urban locality creating and maintaining its own shape against all odds. Ever since the time of the Romans it has been essentially an open space. Admittedly, it has been invaded again and again over the centuries by buildings, some lasting many, many years but somehow all destined to disappear. The Blitz of 1940 finally cleared the area, opening up the western part so that the Tower again looms, dominant. It must be admitted that the immediate approaches to one of Britain's greatest historical monuments leaves much to be desired, for while the overall layout is dignified the temporary stalls for food and drink are out of keeping with the locality and the area is usually liberally garnished with rubbish.

But the pedestrian approach to the Tower of London from the underground railway station is as dramatic as one could wish. Emerging from the noncommittal station, the visitor immediately encounters that great stretch of Roman wall, rearing up as it has done for 2,000 years. The underpass, built in 1979 under the vast new road that bisects Tower Hill, follows the line the Roman wall would have taken and comes out at the postern gate, which disappeared in a subsidence in 1440 and was discovered unexpectedly when the underpass was built. By turning right past the remains of the postern gate, the modern visitor enters Londinium exactly as his predecessors would have done centuries upon centuries ago.

The scaffold upon which so many hundreds rendered up their lives is now represented by a simple, paved area – appropriately enough next to the great monument to the merchant seamen dead in two world wars. Standing on the site of the scaffold and looking down towards the river and the great castle is to go back in time, to see written in one tremendous sweep 1,000 years of history of a great nation. This, too, is the 'nature of the Hill'.

Appendix

A Note on Public Access to the Tower

The public is admitted to the Ceremony of the Keys, which takes place every day at 9.45pm and ends exactly at 10pm. In order to attend it is necessary to make formal application to the Governor by post, when an invitation card will be sent, specifying the date and time of attending. The delay is only a matter of days in winter, but can be prolonged during the high season, for numbers are, naturally, limited.

No formality is needed to attend the Sunday morning service at St Peter ad Vincula as this is a parish church. The would-be visitor should present himself/herself at the Middle Tower (the main entrance to the castle) and state the intention of attending the service. It is inadvisable to stray off the direct route between the Middle Tower and the chapel – which, in any case, passes through the historic heart of the place.

The Tower authorities are gradually opening up more and more of the castle to the public but some of the most interesting apartments still remain out of bounds and are likely to do so in the foreseeable future. These include the entire range of the Queen's House (the old Lieutenant's Lodgings) and St Thomas's Tower (Traitors' Gate) which are both used for residential purposes. Entrance to the Bell Tower, with its cells occupied by More and Fisher as well as many other distinguished prisoners, is through the Queen's House and there is therefore no public access. There is a possibility that the Cradle Tower, with a reconstructed 'cradle' will be opened to the public at some period and there seems no reason why the upper chamber of the Byward Tower, with its recently discovered murals and massive working portcullis machinery, should not also be opened on a controlled basis.

BIBLIOGRAPHY

Virtually any history of England will carry references to the Tower of London, and conversely, any history of the Tower of London will reflect English history. In this luxuriant jungle of books, the author of the present work found the following of particular relevance and value. Although most are out of print, all should be available through ordinary libraries.

For London generally, Stow's invaluable sixteenth-century *Survey* is available in many editions. *Roman London* by Peter Marsden (1980) readably summarizes current archaeological information. *A History of London* by Robert Gray (1978) covers 2,000 years of history for the layperson.

Sir Charles Oman's *History of the Art of War in the Middle Ages* (1924) throws light on Norman tactics and strategy. D F Renn's *Norman Castles in Britain* (1973) puts the Tower in perspective. J H Harvey's *The Medieval Architect* (1972) describes building techniques. H M Colvin's *The History of the King's Works* (1963–70) is a magisterial account of royal castles. The Royal Commission on Historical Monuments's *An Inventory of the Historical Monuments of London*, Vol V (1930), though dated, contains a full 'nuts and bolts' description of the Tower.

Derek Wilson's *The Tower 1078–1978* (1978), published to mark the castle's 900th anniversary, comes as near as possible to a comprehensive history. The standard work is still J Bayley's *The History and Antiquities of the Tower of London* (1830). Harrison Ainsworth's *The Tower of London* (1840) though unabashed fiction with melodramatic set-pieces, contains good background information. R Sutherland Gower's *The Tower of London* (1901–2) and A L Rowse's *The Tower of London in the History of the Nation* (1972) specifically link the castle to English history.

John Gerard's *Autobiography of an Elizabethan* has been translated from the Latin by Philip Caraman with an introduction by Graham Greene (1972). Edward Edwards's *The Life of Sir Walter Ralegh* (1868) provides a good description of Raleigh's imprisonment in the Bloody Tower. Lawrence Tanner and William Wright's *Recent investigation regarding the fate of the Princes in the Tower* was published by the Society of Antiquaries in 1935. Elizabeth Jenkins's *The Princes in the Tower* (1978) accepts that Richard was the murderer while Phillip Lindsay's *King Richard III* (1933) arraigns Henry VII. More's account of the tragedy is in *The English Works of Sir T. More* edited by W E Campbell (1933). *The Official Diary of Lieutenant-General Adam Williamson 1722–1747* was published by the Royal Historical Society (Camden Third Series Vol XXII, 1912).

The Tower of London by Major-General Sir George Younghusband, *His Majesty's Tower of London* by Colonel E H Carkeet-James (1950) and *The Tower of London* by Kenneth J Mears (1988) are all by officers of the Tower. *The Tower of London: its Buildings and Institutions*, edited by John Charlton (1978), is a collection of academic monographs describing various functions, officials and institutions in the Tower. Doyne C Bell's *Notices of the Historic Persons buried in the Chapel of St Peter ad Vincula* (1877) describes the Victorian investigation. The Tower publishes its own guidebooks including a 'souvenir' type by Peter Hammond (1987), and an academic architectural survey by R Allen Brown and P E Curnow (1984) as well as guides to the collections. There is no comprehensive guide to the graffiti but *Inscriptions* by Sarah Barter (1976) describes the more important.

The History of All Hallows Barking by Joseph Maskell (1864) is still the standard work on the church of All Hallows. The LCC *Survey of London* Vols XII and XV (1929) covers Tower Hill and the church. J G Broodbank's *History of the Port of London* (1921) puts the Hill in perspective as London's port while P B Clayton and B R Leftwich's *The Pageant of Tower Hill* (1933) is a mixture of history and contemporary observation. A well-illustrated booklet by Philip Blewett, *All Hallows by the Tower of London* (nd but 1980s), picks out highlights in the ancient church's history.

INDEX

The page numbers of pictures are shown in *italics*.

ACKNOWLEDGEMENTS

The publishers would like to thank the following for supplying illustrations.

Colour

ET Archive, jacket back (above left); Her Majesty's Stationery Office, pages 104 (left and right), 105 (left). All other colour pictures supplied by Simon McBride.

Black and white

Board of Trustees Royal Armouries, page 99 (above and below); BBC Hulton Picture Library, page 122; British Library, pages 38, 39, 42, 44, 48, 60 (right); British Tourist Authority, pages 7, 11, 84, 98; Crown Copyright, reproduced by permission of the Controller of Her Majesty's Stationery Office, page 31, 105 (right); Department of the Environment, 79 (right); ET Archive, pages 67, 78 (above left), 79 (left), 86, 102 (left); Fotomas Index, pages 60 (left), 76; Simon McBride, pages 34, 51, 70 (above and below); National Portrait Gallery, pages 32, 50, 52, 54, 62, 64, 69, 78 (below right), 92, 93, 95; Peter Jackson Collection, frontispiece, pages 66, 94, 102 (right), 103, 106 (right and left); Popperfoto, pages 118, 119; Society of Antiquaries of London, page 33; Wallace Collection, page 90.

THE
TOWER
OF
LONDON

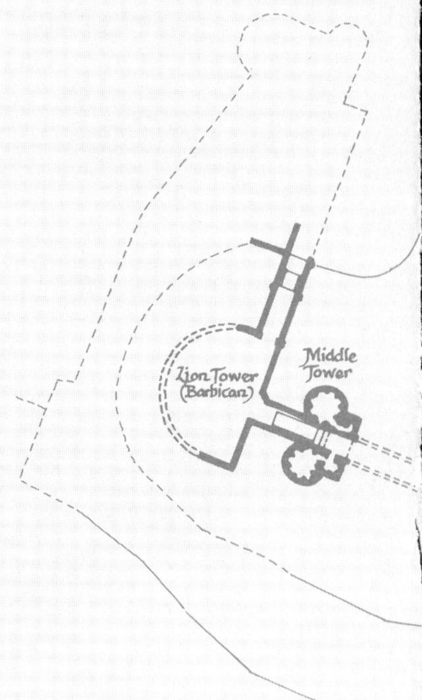
Middle Tower
Lion Tower (Barbican)

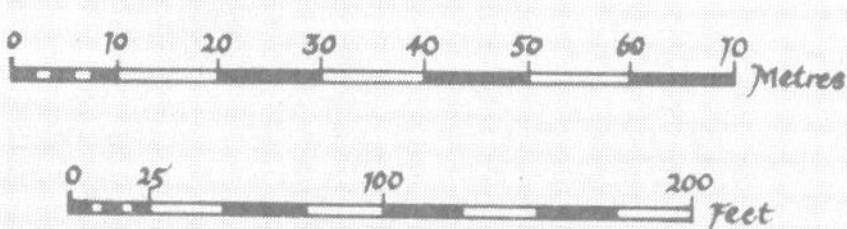
0 10 20 30 40 50 60 70 Metres
0 25 100 200 Feet

RIVER TH